Praise for Mary Wine's *Let Me Love You*

"Sensual, evocative. Not to miss."

~ *Lora Leigh, New York Times Best selling author*

5 Klovers! "Mary Wine's writing is absolutely stellar. She infuses her story effortlessly with all the elements necessary to draw her readers in to the story from the very first chapter – danger, romance, suspense, and a just the right amount of sensual heat..."

~ *Jennifer, ck2s Kwips and Kritiques*

Let Me Love You

Mary Wine

A Samhain Publishing, Ltd. publication.

Samhain Publishing, Ltd.
577 Mulberry Street, Suite 1520
Macon, GA 31201
www.samhainpublishing.com

Editing by Anne Scott
Cover by Vanessa Hawthorne

First Samhain Publishing, Ltd. electronic publication: July 2007
First Samhain Publishing, Ltd. print publication: May 2008

Chapter One

"This here is a man's world, honey. It's time you got that into your pretty head."

The main difficulty Brianna had with Joseph Corners' words was the fact that the man was saying "head" when his gaze was very definitely on her chest. Actually, the man was staring at her bosom, but noticing such a vulgar detail sort of cast her into the gutter along with Joseph.

At least that's what Brianna's mother would have said. Ladies didn't think about their bosoms, even if they were being ogled in the bright light of day. But maybe those lessons were better suited to the streets of Boston, instead of the dock in Silver Peak, California.

Joseph sniffed before stepping closer. "Will you marry me?"

Nausea threatened to send her lunch up as an answer to Joseph's proposal. He grinned and the expression showed off his yellow teeth. Several days' growth of beard decorated his chin and his hair looked like she could grease her boots with it. His shirt was sporting splotches from his last few meals and the tail hung free of his trousers. While the West might be untamed, somehow

Brianna couldn't quite take courtship from a slob seriously. You could admire a man who worked hard all day. If it was sweat and honest labor that stained his clothing that might be a point in his favor. But no woman wanted a lazy man in her house. All that promised was a life of hardship with an empty belly. There wasn't a single thing about Joseph that even came close to the idea of likeable.

She was no picture of pristine beauty either, with a day's work behind her, but there was a difference between the stains of honest labor sitting on a man and pure gluttony.

A thin coating of flour that she couldn't seem to shake off clung to her skirt. Brianna worked in a mill her father had built in the little town of Silver Peak. The huge stone-grinding mill was powered by a waterwheel set on the edge of the river. The local farmers were eager to have their crop ground into flour that could be sold right there in any of the mining towns, instead of carting their crops to an eastern market.

"Now, Mr. Corners, I have quite clearly explained to you that you must speak to my father." But she'd rather be shipped to a convent if it meant avoiding a meeting at the church altar with Joseph Corners. The idea of enduring his kiss made her shiver and clamp her lips closed against a second round of nausea. She'd just bet his breath was worse than old fish.

Joseph spat on the ground as he stepped closer. Brianna backed up but looked around the man for any sign of anyone else. She was walking down the river dock and, although daylight, it wasn't exactly a proper place for a lady to be. She had an account to settle with the dock master and the amount was large or she never would have risked some of the more unsavory elements you could count on meeting.

"Your father is dead." Joseph wiped his hand on the top of his forearm. "Everyone knows it. It's time you married up and let a man run that mill." Joseph made a grab for her and moved rather fast for his plump belly. His fingers curled around her wrist, his fingers digging in like a hawk catching a mouse, pinching her limb and sending pain shooting up into her shoulder.

"Release me, sir."

A snicker was her reply. Joseph actually licked his lower lip as he dragged her forward. Her boots skidded on the rough plank deck as she thrust out her opposite arm to keep herself from tumbling into his stained shirt. A shudder shook her frame as she envisioned herself held in his embrace. Getting shoved into the river sounded more appealing.

The sunlight flickered as something blocked it for a brief second.

"Release the lady and stand aside, Mr. Corners."

Brianna gasped and Joseph cussed as a man stepped into their sight. A shotgun leaned against the man's shoulder and his finger rested on the trigger. He was a huge man with shoulders that filled out his duster. Brianna stared at the black coat because the color was expensive. Most men didn't lay down the coin for a black coat when an undyed garment would do the same job of cutting the night chill and keeping the rain off their skin. The type of men that paid for black oil cloth dusters were the sort who didn't want to be seen at night.

"Get lost. Me and the lady are busy." Joseph's voice didn't sound very steady as he puffed up his chest. But while he was distracted, his grip slackened allowing her to yank her arm out of his hand.

The stranger followed her with his gaze as she placed a couple of large steps between herself and Joseph. Her would-be suitor growled under his breath and raised both his hands before moving towards her.

"You have one thing right, she is a lady." The stranger's gaze touched her face briefly before settling back on Joseph. His expression was etched in stone as he glared at the slob trying to court her.

A blush warmed her cheeks, as she listened to the title of respect. The eyes on this man were so intense she felt them when they moved over her. A little ripple of awareness traveled across her skin as she watched their company take another step towards them.

"And the lady told you to go find her father. I suggest you do it. Now. Because I'm not as polite as the lady is."

It was the strangest thing to notice, but the stranger never raised his voice. He kept it low and steady. Even she was compelled to straighten her back just a bit in response to the authority in his rich tone. It practically radiated from him. Like heat did on a hot day. Even after sunset you could place your hand on a rock and still feel the blazing power of the noon sun.

"And I told you to get lost—"

The man moved like a rattlesnake, fast and deadly. Hard fingers closed around her wrist and a quick jerk sent her body stumbling behind his. The rifle that had lain so harmlessly against his shoulder was now leveled with a firm hand. Joseph cussed again, but he shuffled backwards across the dusty dock as the muzzle of the weapon settled even with his belly.

"Your conversation with the lady is finished."

The look on Joseph's face said something completely different, but along with his sloppiness went a good dose of cowardice. Somehow, Brianna got the feeling the stranger wouldn't have backed down from something he wanted, even in the face of a loaded rifle. She wasn't too sure which side to bet on—the gun or the man holding it. While the rifle was the respected law of the West, she got the notion the man holding it could and would deal with Joseph without the weapon if he needed to. It was almost a polite way of running Joseph off, using the muzzle of the rifle. A little shiver worked its way over her skin as she detected all the subtle hints of a man that could use his body as a weapon when he was of a mind to do so. It was a mark of his strength, because Silver Peak was full of men who let their bodies run to fat while they relied on guns to protect themselves and their property. They paid the less fortunate to do their labor while gorging on their profits and being lazy.

She considered the man in front of her for a long moment and found all the things that she'd noticed lacking in Joseph. This stranger's shirt was marked slightly with dirt, but each button was set through its hole neatly, while the tail was tucked down into his pants with a wide belt buckled in place around his waist. His pants weren't new, but they had been washed recently. Even his boots looked well kept beneath a fresh layer of dust. There were few paved roads in Silver Peak, and only in the very center of the town. That meant most of the inhabitants polished their shoes every day or ended up looking like Joseph. The two men were polar opposites.

"It ain't finished." Joseph spat before his attention centered on her breasts again. Something flickered in his eyes and it made her feel dirty just being touched by his gaze. Shifting farther behind the back of her unexpected savior felt almost necessary, even if she was acting the fool.

She didn't know anything about him either. It was a blunt fact that she held a better chance of dealing with Joseph than the black-clad man. He might just be running Joseph off in order to set himself up with a clear chance at her.

The good Lord knew that would just fit with her recent run of luck.

But a part of her cringed at the thought of him being disreputable. She found herself wanting to believe in that deep rich voice. Even if it was just a little flight of fantasy. It had been a long time since she'd enjoyed any bit of imagination. It had also been far too long since she'd felt even a morsel of trust stir for anyone. With her father away, practicality had forced her to view everyone with suspicion. Whoever he was, the man in front of her tempted her to trust him. Keep faith in his word and his morals long enough to relax for a moment, instead of worrying about what he might try and take from her when she wasn't watching.

With the number of days mounting up since her sire's departure, she was running dry on keeping ahead of folks like Joseph who wanted to scoop up the mill. There were a whole lot of people in Silver Peak who agreed with Joseph about her needing a man around to run things. The banker who held the mortgage on her mill was one of loudest. Telling her to marry up before she lost the only dowry her father had left her. That attitude had sent her down onto the docks because she needed the money owed her to keep her hands on her father's property. She'd done the work, but collecting the fee due her wasn't proving very easy.

But she'd rather walk the dock than down the church aisle. The West wasn't Boston. A woman could shoulder as much as a man as long as she was willing to challenge the rules of society. Taking charge of her unpaid account personally felt just fine to her way of thinking. It wasn't the worst she'd seen. A couple of Marshall Wentworth's daughters had been seen in pants. Not in town, mind you, but another thing Silver Peak hungered for was entertainment, and gossip moved faster than the mail. The Wentworths' ranch was twenty miles outside town. The miners had seen his daughters working in britches alongside the man's sons. While practical, it was also scandalous. The church pews were full of good wives who enjoyed the juicy tidbit.

"It ain't finished by no long shot. You'll wear my ring and warm my bed."

Joseph's words slapped her back to reality. The anger in his voice was harsh, but the lust burning in his eyes was sickening. He raked her body with one last gaze before he hitched his sagging britches up and left. Relief lasted a mere second before her rescuer turned his attention to her. Dark and as hard as obsidian, his gaze inspected her. She couldn't gain a hint of his mood from his expression. One of his hands rose to the brim of his hat. He touched it in a quick gesture of respect that she hadn't been expecting, even if he did call her a lady.

It had been a long time since anyone made her feel respected.

"Miss Spencer, I believe you need to take your afternoon stroll down the main street. The docks are no place for a lady."

He didn't raise his voice but that didn't mask his disapproval. Her pride reared its head in the face of being chastised like some debutante without her chaperone. Her chin rose as her hands settled on her hips. The stance was habit, learned while standing her ground when customers thought they could cheat her just because she wasn't wearing a pair of britches.

With her father still missing, it was up to her to pay the yearly balance or watch everything go up on the auction block. No way she was going to disappoint her daddy. He'd placed a roof over her head for twenty years. It seemed only fair that she helped keep it there now that he needed her help. She wouldn't stand by while the vultures converged on their hard-earned possessions.

"I'm collecting an account from the dock master. Afternoon strolls are for the privileged. I earn my way in this world, sir."

Something flickered in his obsidian eyes. The rifle lay against his shoulder once again, but this time she wasn't fooled by the ease with which he handled it. This man was deadly. He was the worst kind of hunter, the sort who looked harmless right up until he struck.

"Clayton owes you?"

His gaze moved over her, missing nothing. Heat surged through her veins and it had nothing to do with the afternoon sun. It was the honest truth that the wind was bitter, snow on its edge. She shied away from placing a label on the reason her cheeks burned. His attention settled on the scarlet staining her face. His lips pressed tighter into a hard line before he forced his eyes to meet hers. He moved one side of the dark duster and a silver badge flashed in the sunlight. The railroad agent badge was a symbol of authority on the docks. While one side of the docks was used by the river barges, the railroad was set right on the other side of the planks. It was the main artery that allowed Silver Peak to breathe. The barges brought goods up the river and the trains carried everything else in and out of town. That made it more important than the bank. There was more money sitting out under the sun than locked away in the center of town. Railroad agents protected the interests of the railroad by making sure their payloads didn't go missing from the docks. The rifle lying against his hard shoulder suddenly made perfect sense. He was on duty and that meant something valuable was nearby. Something men would risk their lives to steal.

"Clayton still owes you for the grain he had ground two months ago?"

The heat in her face doubled as she was forced to admit to a stranger how long the account had gone uncollected. Clayton's men had hauled off his order and snickered as they left her dirty from four weeks of work and with no pay.

"I'm certain the matter has simply slipped his mind. Dock master is a demanding position in the spring and summer." It hadn't slipped the man's mind, but she wasn't going to admit she had been taken for a fool. Next season it would be half down or no grinding. Even the Chinese were savvy enough to demand half payment upfront. Well, if it was good enough for the Chinese, it was good enough for her.

"I'll make certain Clayton gets the message. You have a nice day."

His voice told her the conversation was finished. The badge winking at her in the winter sunlight backed up his ability to evict her from the dock. Railroad agents held the authority to lock the area down. She didn't like it. Clayton owed her a debt. A part of her wanted to face the man down. She knew he was hiding on his docks because he thought she was too chicken to march up to his office and demand settlement. The church pews would be buzzing about her conduct this Sunday, but she wasn't sorry. Sometimes you had to do something that the rest of the world didn't agree with. That was just life on the frontier.

"No need. I'll attend to the matter when the docks are open again."

Brianna dropped him a tiny curtsy before turning and walking away. Surprise broke his expressionless mask for a brief second, but that moment was etched in her mind. Satisfaction filled her as she moved back towards her horse. No, she didn't need a man to run her father's mill.

And that would make Gregory Spencer right proud of his only child. She might be a daughter, but she was pure Spencer blood. Yeah, her daddy would be proud, wherever he was. She hugged that knowledge tight to her heart as she refused to consider any of the nasty fates that might have claimed her father. He wasn't dead. She'd feel it in her soul if he was. So, she was going to make certain her father's mill was waiting for him when he made it home. No Spencer gave up so easily. Since she was her father's only child, it doubled her duty to hold the family name up. He'd only been missing since spring. There were any number of reasons why his hunting trip had prevented him from coming home. His horse might have gone lame and everybody knew you had to tend to an injured mount, because a horse was essential in the West. She'd bet he'd written her a letter and it just hadn't reached her. Well, the mail was as uncertain as the supply wagons. Maybe he was tending to his horse up in the woods where there wasn't any way to get a letter into circulation.

No, her father wasn't dead and she refused to even entertain that it was a possibility. She'd think of three more reasons that might be delaying him instead. Positive attitude was the key. Yes, it was.

Sloan McAlister watched Brianna leave. He shouldn't have. His attention lingered on the sway of her hips in a blunt form of appreciation that was guaranteed to land him in trouble. Considering the worn calico of her dress, he was a bastard for eyeing her. There was a twitch from his cock that capitalized the word "bastard", but it wasn't enough to make him turn away. Lady or not, he enjoyed the view. It was far from polite, but it was honest.

He always had been a sucker for a woman with spunk. The problem was that of the two sorts of women a man had to choose from, spunk tended to live in the wild ones. In the West, that meant the saloon girls who took life by the throat with one hand firmly clasped around its testicles. They were merciless females who earned fortunes by dangling their flesh in front of hungry miners as they milked those men of their newly discovered gold. Truly savvy women could spend a couple of years on their backs and earn enough to return east and live well. Sin often paid better than respectable employment—it always had.

Brianna Spencer wasn't that sort. No, she was a lady. No doubt about it. He'd bet his right arm that she was wearing a pair of knickers beneath her calico and petticoat. Under that intimate garment would be a sweet channel that she'd never let a man touch. She wouldn't sell it for anything less than a man's vow in front of a parson.

It had been a long time since he'd been so close to a female he managed to respect. Sure, the town was full of virginal daughters and church-going mothers, but they were just as petty as the gold prospectors. They hunted husbands in the same cold-blooded manner. He'd had a taste of their respectable dealings before and knew better than to walk anywhere near their church hall socials. He wasn't considered husband material, but his badge was used as a shield to allow their daughters to practice their charms on him. Holding the position of an agent only meant the good mothers of the town expected him to take their teasing until a proper suitor stepped up. Being used never sat well with him, so he avoided the "good" folk in town.

Brianna wasn't that kind. She was a rare sort of woman who enjoyed knowing she made her way in the world without compromise. That was something else he liked too much in a female.

Independence.

A lot of men got that confused with a blow to their pride, but Sloan didn't see it the same. A woman who faced life with a healthy dose of self-confidence in her own ability was usually fire between the sheets.

His cock hardened and he cussed softly under his breath. He was sure a dumb ass tonight. Letting his mind wander over the thighs of a woman like Brianna would only gain him a cock that wasn't going to be satisfied with a whore.

Well, at least he had a fine target for his foul temper. Turning, he moved across the dock towards Clayton's office. It wasn't his duty to deal with the man, but he couldn't resist the idea of seeing her once more. Besides, he didn't like sharing his dock with a crook or knowing that his supply cupboard had unpaid flour in it. The dock master stocked the agents' bunkhouse and was paid by the company for the goods. Clayton was double dealing. As long as Sloan was on duty, the matter was going to be settled to his personal satisfaction.

Rattling Brianna Spencer sounded like a better reason to confront Clayton though.

That was another fault of his, pulling tails just to watch the fire dance. His mood darkened dangerously. He wanted to see flames dance in Brianna's eyes. The kind no man had the right to associate with any lady of her caliber. But that didn't change the heat that raced through his erect cock or the hunger rising inside him to be the man to taste her.

Or maybe the word was tempt. He certainly was tempted and he'd always figured that payback was fair play.

Except this kind of game left burns that scarred. Her face was already etched into his mind and he got the feeling she was going to dance through his dreams, too. Even that made his lips twitch. A man couldn't really complain about a dream that featured Brianna. He might cuss but he wouldn't complain. There were a lot worse things his memory could choose to taunt him with during the night. Brianna's sweet swaying hips were a far cry better than a few deeds that decorated his past. Maybe that was the reason he savored the swollen erection with a half grin sitting on his lips. His life was hard, but today it had offered up a sweet little ray of delight.

It was worth whipping Clayton into line.

CR

As the sun set, the temperature dropped quickly. Brianna rushed through her final chores and hurried back to warm herself in front of her stove. It was time to pull out her flannel petticoat. The season for lightweight cotton was gone. Ice was appearing on the edges of the river each morning as winter loomed over Silver Peak.

The two-room cabin her father had built when he brought her west was attached to the grinding house. Two small rooms, constructed to minimize the amount of coal they needed to heat the dwelling in winter. She'd never minded the humbleness of the dwelling. Even if it was a stark contrast to the house she'd lived in back in Virginia. Home wasn't a place, but more of a feeling. It was the people who lived there with you that made it a sanctuary from the rest of the world. Her daddy had always been all the security she needed.

A little mutter of sorrow passed her lips as she poked at the coals in the stove. Heat hit her face and she smiled as it warmed her chilled nose. White snow would blanket the ground in the morning, but her bed would be cozy due to her father's wisdom in making the mill house small. His double bed was in the same room as the stove. The back one had been hers, added on one spring before the ice broke over the river and grinding could begin again. There was a tiny stove in it as well, but she'd shut the door firmly against the cold and taken to sleeping in the main cabin since her father had been gone. It would be foolish to waste money on heating her room when she kept the main stove fired for cooking. With the bank note looming over her, every penny was precious.

Closing the side door of the stove, she turned her attention to the cast-iron pot sitting on the back of it. Wrapping a folded cloth over the handle, she pulled the lid up with a curved iron hook. Her dinner smelled delightful as she gave it a turn with a large copper spoon. Working the mill meant she had to be clever enough to set her nightly meal to simmering in the morning or she ate cold supper at night. Halting work to check on her meal wasn't a very effective business strategy. More than one man in town had resorted to a mail-order bride just to share the workload. In the West, it took a devoted couple to keep a house running with any degree of comfort. Romance took a second-row seat to the harsher reality of having the cupboard stocked for winter. A man might bring in the harvest, but needed another set of hands to stew it down and set it into jars so it might soothe the belly during the bitter months. The town parson was fond of reminding his flock just how comfortable life was when a man married up and shared the workload. The reverend was another person who would like to see her wed. At least he had heavenly reasoning.

A little giggle escaped her lips as she considered just what a church wedding would lead to—a consummation. Joseph wanted her in his bed, too, and it was rather funny when you recognized that everyone's ideas would see her warming a man's bed. It was wicked of her to place both parson and Joseph in the same group but it was still amusing when she considered that sex was going to be the end result of both ideas.

"You're a shame, Brianna." Muttering to herself, she turned back towards the chore of cooking supper.

The remains of a ham shank coupled with kidney beans and dried peas had stewed up over the dying coals quite nicely. After dropping freshly mixed biscuit dough into it, she placed the cover on top and waited for the dumplings to cook. The thick, black cast iron of the pot was hot and it wouldn't take long.

The chill in the air made her shudder as she opened the door to her pantry. She considered the rows of neatly stored jars of fruit she'd spent endless hours preserving for the coming winter. Even the autumn pomegranates were gone now. She counted the jars and sighed at the number. Working alone, she'd only managed to put up a portion of what she had the year past. She'd burned a lot of oil in order to do it, too, because she couldn't stand at the stove and grind grain at the same time. Large families were another thing westerners welcomed. It meant lots of hands to help with the workload.

Winter could be long and bitter. You learned to sleep less during the summer so that you didn't starve when the snow drifted past your door. Two large sacks of apples caught her eye. Reaching inside one, she pulled out a slightly wizened piece of fruit. A few customers paid their fees in food. She'd forgotten about the apples as the last rush of the season kept her at the grinding stone until late. The daytime temperatures had been too warm to keep the apples sitting in her pantry firm. If they froze below ground in her root cellar, they'd become mushy. Apple pie was only a treat for the summer because, in Silver Peak, it was apple cider or preserves the rest of the year. Her cider press was out back of the mill house in the chill of the night. A little shiver shook her as she considered working the large corkscrew iron press. Hot cider might fill her kitchen with a sweet scent near Christmas when she was starving for some cheer, but it didn't fill the belly very effectively.

Preserves would smell just as nice and make a fine tart for the Yuletide season. The snow might be too deep for her to attend church on Christmas or for that matter a good portion of the month. There would be no trip to the mercantile to fill her empty pantry. Besides, the bank note would be due again come spring. Better to keep her fist tight around every coin until the land note was paid in full. It was a dream that shimmered in her imagination, as well as in many of her neighbors'.

Picking up the burlap bag, she hummed as she returned to the stove and dropped it in easy reach. Her Dutch oven cast-iron pot was waiting on the sideboard. Her cooking ware was worth a great deal. The bigger iron kettle had been bought just last year. Her father had insisted on purchasing it when he'd caught her drooling over its two-gallon size. Larger pots were rare in the territories; every one had to be shipped in from the east. With its size she could stew down a large batch, saving time. She counted it a blessing this season because her smaller pot would never have gotten her the number of jars she had in the pantry.

"Thanks, Daddy."

Reaching for a knife, she began to chop and slice the fruit as her supper simmered. The kitchen soon smelled like cinnamon and sugar as she splurged on her last preserving project of the season by opening up her spice jar. It was a perfect touch for a chilly night. A kerosene lamp cast a yellow glow over her labor as she mixed up a small tin of cobble crust to bake a little treat for herself while the rest of the apples stewed down so that she could store them away in jars.

A hard knock landed on the front door, shattering her bliss. She stared at the sturdy bar she had in place as a second pounding hit the wood. She peeked through the curtain and dropped the fabric as she saw a shadowy form in a black duster standing on her front step. Just enough light was spilling out from her window to illuminate the face of the railroad agent. Brianna frowned at the glass pane. Her pretty summer calico curtain let the light spill right out onto her front step, announcing the fact that she was home. With the entire town knowing she lived alone, it was a foolish lapse in forethought. Tomorrow, she was going to nail the storm shutters closed.

But that wasn't going to solve her dilemma tonight.

"Oh, honestly!"

She put her stirring spoon down and went towards the door. Turning into a frightened mouse sure wasn't going to do her any good. If the man intended to harm her, he'd smash the little kitchen window quite easily. Since he was knocking, she might as well answer the door.

Glass was really expensive and she had to live in the house once he'd finished his business. Whatever it might be. Besides, working herself into a fit of fear was only going to keep her from gaining a good night's rest because her mind was chasing phantoms instead of slumbering.

He touched his hat again as she let the full light from her lamp illuminate him. Even when she stood a full step higher than him, he still rose above her. A tiny flicker of amusement filled his eyes as she pushed the door wide open, instead of hiding behind it as if it were some kind of shield. She might be a fool, but she wasn't a coward.

"Good evening, Miss Spencer."

His voice was deep and controlled, exactly the way she remembered it. A ripple of excitement moved through her, touching off a little wave of apprehension. She wasn't starved for company so that wasn't the reason her heart picked up its pace in the face of her caller. His attention wavered as she noticed him taking a deep breath. The stewing cinnamon had met with his approval as well. Her pride blossomed as she watched a flare of appreciation cross his eyes. Improper or not, she enjoyed seeing that her cooking met with his favor.

Brianna frowned as she realized that the snow was already falling. The black duster was wet across his shoulders from the delicate flakes landing and melting against his body heat. She pushed the door wide in invitation. He frowned at her and shook his head.

"I don't think so. Just came by to deliver Clayton's response to your visit."

His voice was hard. Brianna felt her pride stir again as she rested one hand on her hip. "I keep a decent house, Mr. McAlister. No need to stand in the snow."

One side of his mouth twitched. It didn't actually form into a grin, but a sparkle in his eyes said he was amused by her offended pride. Only in the untamed West would she have offered to let any man into her home and maybe she was an idiot for doing it. But impulses rarely made any sense. Besides, it was practical. All her heat was escaping.

"That wasn't a slight to your housekeeping skills." He considered her for a long moment. "But you knew that, didn't you?"

A husky chuckle was her response as she left the doorway and returned to her stove. "Maybe I did, but it seems rather silly to stand in the cold when I'm spending the coin on good coal." A little chill moved down her spine as she turned her back on him. Her body was all flushed again, excitement racing along her limbs like a child anticipating Christmas morning.

Actually, it was deeper than that and there was nothing childish about the sensation. A hard ache centered in her belly as she felt him step into the cabin. She hadn't counted on the way the room shrank once he was in it. A wave of vulnerability swept through her as she felt her nipples tingle. It was disturbing how aware she suddenly was of her body. No man had ever interested her in such a fashion before.

"Your father should have broken you of that tendency to toy with fire."

She peeked over her shoulder at him and shrugged. Her eyelashes fluttered with a coy motion before she twisted her lips into a sarcastic smile. "I invited you in out of the snow, Mr. McAlister. If you take that as anything more, the fault lies in you."

He groaned, low and deep, and she flinched at the sound. Her face went smooth as she looked at him with pure surprise. Uncertain how to deal with the male reaction she began to chew her lower lip.

His dark gaze lowered to her teeth, watching the nervous motion. There were a few things in life that no soul alive could fake. Experience with the opposite sex was one of them. She'd exhausted her meager confidence when it came to dealing with a full-grown man.

"Clayton's answer."

Reaching into his duster pocket, he pulled a small cloth bag out. Taking one step into the cabin, he offered it to her.

She lifted a pot lid instead, unwilling to give him a reason to leave so soon. The rich scent of stewing apples floated towards the open door and she heard his stomach rumble. The little bag offered her an end to weeks of worry over the bank note. Even if he was a stranger, currently he qualified as her best friend.

She laughed as he continued to frown at her. "You might as well stay for supper. Since you're here."

"What the hell are you doing asking a man to supper?" He slapped the bag Clayton had tied his payment into on the little table as he glared at her. "I could be the meanest bastard in these hills. You should have left the bar across the door."

"It wouldn't have done much good."

She turned and propped her hands on her hips. The challenge in his voice rubbed her temper. Pointing her spoon at the window, she watched his face register understanding. "I'll be nailing those shutters closed tomorrow, but seeing as how you're here tonight, not being pleasant wouldn't make much difference if you were intent on having your way."

Brianna sighed. She was so tired of the struggle! That constant need to put up a strong front. It had been too long since she'd been pleasant for the sake of being neighborly. Even manners were considered a sign of weakness on the frontier. It made her head ache. But a little twist of regret went through her heart as well. The man in front of her was the kind she just might be interested in displaying some tiny bit of ladylike grace for. Maybe it was the badge he wore, but she couldn't shake the idea that he was a man of principle. That badge told her he was dedicated to something more than seeking out his own fortune. All too rare in Silver Peak. It was an affliction the West suffered from—greedy men. A girl had to be careful she didn't end up hitched to a man who only wanted her dowry. More than one woman had found herself abandoned when the money ran dry and her belly swelled up with a responsibility her new husband wasn't going to shoulder.

He suddenly closed the gap between them. He stepped right up and brushed her body with his. It was a mere whisper of a touch, but it stung like a hot ember. She jumped away from his imposing figure. He was too hard and male. The need to escape pounded through her without granting her any room for thought. She simply reacted.

He jerked her to a halt before she collided with the stove. One arm slipped around her waist and pulled her back against his body. A firm hand cupped her chin and raised it until their gazes connected. His obsidian eyes were ablaze with heat and it sent a shudder through her as he let his gaze settle on her lips for a long moment.

She hung between the desire for a kiss and the fear that he would press his mouth against hers. She actually doubted her own desire to push him away if he did kiss her. Temptation slithered through her mind, pulling her towards the idea of indulging in one stolen moment while no one was around to witness her recklessness. Her cheeks colored with that knowledge. She'd never been the sort of woman tempted by lust, but at that moment her entire body was a mass of quivering sensation that clamored for his kiss.

And she didn't even know the man's name.

He stroked her blush-stained cheek with a single finger. The skin-to-skin contact raced down her neck and beneath her corset where her nipples were still drawn into tight little points. Her heart was racing and her quickened breaths drew his male scent deep into her lungs. Her belly tightened as his gaze moved back to hers. Hard hunger flickered in those obsidian depths and it scared her as much as it excited her. His embrace was unbreakable, but all that did was add excitement to the moment.

"Nail your shutters shut and never trust a man again."

He turned her body around and let her go. She stumbled back and her temper flared as she hit the table. But the retort bubbling up her throat died before crossing her lips as she caught the look he cast her. Something untamed stared back at her. Fear of him didn't make her hold her tongue. Pure fascination with the flare of uncivilized maleness flickering in his gaze did. It excited her to see such heat aimed at her. Never once had she considered herself alluring.

Shame turned her face bright red. "You're a harsh man." And the worst part was the fact that she liked it all too much.

"Keeps me alive." He stepped out her front door a second later. He dragged a deep breath into his lungs before he touched the brim of his wide Stetson. "Sloan McAlister. Pleasure helping you collect your account."

She slammed the door in his face. Sloan grinned at the worn wood as he heard the bar being shoved into place. His stomach rumbled and he tried to think about the meal she'd offered him and just how damn long it had been since he'd eaten anything as fine as her home cooking smelled.

But his mind didn't stay on his stomach. His thoughts homed in on the real hunger he wanted to feed and that had nothing to do with the cinnamon drifting on the night air. It ran a hell of a lot deeper. Snaking through his flesh to the hard erection in the front of his britches. His gaze moved to the window as his thoughts told him just how simple it would be to get her back into his arms.

Clayton's payment still sat on her table. That little bundle of temptation that gave him the chance to seek her out when he knew damn good and well he had no business sniffing around her. He lived his life with a rifle on his shoulder. That cut respectable women out clean. Besides, the sort of entertainment he craved went beyond wifely duty. It was dark, and sometimes harsh, but polite compliance between the sheets wasn't his idea of marriage.

He turned and strode into the cold night to where his horse was tethered to a tree. Swinging up into the saddle he toyed with that dangerous idea all the way back to town. He tempered his lustful thoughts with iron control, maintaining his course away from Brianna and her fine kitchen. But he still enjoyed the burn of arousal as it tried to eat at his resolve. The personal battle took the edge off his hunger while the chill of approaching winter bit through his duster. Catching the first noise from the saloons as he neared the edge of town, he grunted with satisfaction. Kneeing his horse forward, he forced himself farther from the object of his thoughts. The pianos were busy filling the night with fast music and the promise of quick women. But there wasn't a single madam that interested him. Maybe he was getting old, but laying down with a female who only wanted his money left a bad taste in his mouth. The fragile scent he'd inhaled while Brianna was imprisoned in his embrace burned into his mind as the most potent perfume he'd ever encountered.

He headed back to his dock bunkhouse as he cussed at fate. Brianna's face filled his head, along with the way her body fit against his. She had a little nose and dark blue eyes that hit him as far too cute. That was a word you used to describe girls, not women you wanted to handle. She wasn't beautiful, but he found her incredibly attractive because of her fiery nature. His cock throbbed for more than just ideas, but he grinned as he hung his hat and duster on the hooks next to his door. He snickered at himself as he considered the fact that a female out there could turn his cock hard without lifting her hem to flash her knickers. It sure was a surprise to find Brianna Spencer so difficult to banish from his mind.

Although it might be a long shot, it just might prove that he wasn't past any hope of redemption.

Maybe.

Chapter Two

Sloan McAlister.

Brianna hissed and attacked her morning work with a vengeance that had built up as she'd tossed and kicked through the night. She drove thick iron nails through her window shutters, adding a few new boards to the inside just for good measure. She didn't bother to think about how she was ever going to get them open again.

Sloan McAlister...

Ohhhh! She'd like to say a few well-sharpened words to the man today. Finishing off his visit with an introduction took her beyond infuriated. If he was going to touch her, the least the man could have done was finish the job by kissing her.

A groan surfaced from her throat as she stopped to confront the real reason she was mad. Shame. Thick and hot, she was facing the biggest deviation from the road of straight and narrow she had ever been tempted with. Sins of the flesh had never enticed her before. Her memory taunted her with the way she felt in his embrace. Good saints, she had never even suspected her body could feel so good or so much at one time. The devil sure did bait his trap well, because she was like a fox fixated on fresh meat laid out in a steel trap during the dead of winter. She could smell it and practically taste how good it would be to have Sloan touch his mouth to hers. Even risking the steel jaws of the trap wasn't too much, considering the bait. She hungered for that kiss.

She shivered and then laughed at her own foolish daydreams. She didn't have any clue what a man's kiss was like. That was a hard fact of working every day. Like a lot of folks in the small mining town, even Sunday wasn't a reason to be idle. She wasn't lacking in faith, but piety didn't place food on the supper table. The best bargain she'd come up with was to grind only barter jobs on the Lord's day after church service was done.

However, the workload didn't leave any time for social meetings either. It had been a small eternity since she'd heard music. A lone fiddle would be a feast for her starving senses. Courting was as big a mystery now as it had been when she'd turned fourteen and was considered old enough to receive a gentleman caller.

And now she dreamed of being kissed by Sloan McAlister.

That was a huge blot on her soul, if ever she strayed from the teachings of her mother. Sloan wasn't a gentleman. She could almost hear her mother lecturing on about the proper type of man a lady received. A lady only gave her time to a gentleman who shined his shoes before calling on her. He might bring flowers or some small gift for her mother, but of course a proper suitor never tried to bestow a gift to a lady outright. He would call every Sunday afternoon, in a clean coat, to sit and flirt with her under the supervision of some suitable chaperone. He might kiss her hand, in an ever so soft salute of affection. While they wasted the afternoon with idle chatter. Only their gazes touching, in proper, respectable courtship.

Her lips twitched as she considered the way Sloan had pulled her up against his body last night. Absolutely nothing genteel about it. He'd handled her, like, well she wasn't sure what the phrase was, but he'd handled her. The good matrons in town would tell her he was sin incarnate, if they got wind of it. She could practically hear them berating her with their quotes from the Bible about eternal damnation over admitting that she enjoyed being kissed by Sloan McAlister. No doubt about it, they'd point their fingers and heap guilt onto her head. Warning her to turn her nose up at him or face disgrace.

But that didn't change the fact that her nipples tingled again and she hugged her arms over her chest. Her breasts were sensitive. It was surprising to discover her body alive with enjoyment she hadn't considered before. How exactly did a man tempt a woman with nothing more than a stroke across her cheek?

It baffled her. Just about as much as Sloan intrigued her. Held against his body, she had felt so trapped, but a portion of her enjoyed knowing he was stronger. It was a first in her life. She'd always taken pride in keeping up with her father when the rest of the townsfolk shook their heads and proclaimed it a shame that he didn't have a son, and wasn't it time to remarry?

Her daddy had told her he was still in love with her mother. He was a one-woman man, even if their marriage had ended before his life did. She always loved listening to her father talk about his late wife. His voice still glowed with every sentence as he talked about courting her mother and convincing her to marry up with a man who had little more than a dream to offer her.

A shiver worked its way down her spine. Sloan McAlister wasn't evoking that same sort of warm, secure feeling. She bit into her lip as she pulled the money out of her pantry. Every penny was accounted for. A feat she had to honestly admit she'd have found difficult to accomplish. Clayton had been dodging her for weeks while sending his bullyboys to fetch his ground flour. Two other clients had begun to mimic his behavior since he was getting away with it.

The law was uncertain in any territory town, but the railroad authority was about as solid as it got. Without the railroad, the town would die practically overnight. A man like Sloan held a huge amount of power over men like Clayton who earned their way on the docks. If the agents reported corruption back to their superiors, a rail line might not be used. The residents would have to use their wagons to bring in supplies if the train didn't stop. The railroads owned the rails and only they made the choice on where to stop their trains.

Sure, she might just refuse to grind anything for Clayton, but she risked retaliation. Oh, nothing outright or that could be proved, but she didn't need a run of bad-luck accidents.

Tucking the money into her skirt pocket, she considered her reflection. Her hair was slicked back because of her own sweat and her nose was pasty white with flour. Her breasts with all their new awareness chimed in to tell her that her skin felt grimy. Her brain tempted her with the thought of a bath. With the window nailed firmly shut, she was at liberty to bar the door and strip down for a complete bath.

One thing the back bedroom was good for was bathing. Her old bedroom had also been the washroom. There was a common tin tub, lightweight enough to be brought down river without too much expense. Her father had built a large water tank out back of the cabin. It was on top of sturdy posts that elevated it enough so that when you pulled the piece of wood out of its bottom, gravity let the water rush down and fill the tub. Last night's snow had filled the tub and the afternoon sun had melted a good amount of it by now. There was also a drainpipe set into the wood floor to save her from having to empty dirty water by hand. Baths were not a luxury she got in the dead of winter because the water tank froze over. She'd have to make do with snow that she hauled in a bucket at a time while letting all her coal heat out the front door as she did it.

Filling a kettle, she set it on the stove and barred the door. The idea of being pretty took hold of her and there was no denying she wanted to indulge her feminine side. As long as she was going to town to take Clayton's money to the bank, she might as well look good. Her memory reminded her that it was Friday. A smile covered her face as she began to dig the hairpins out of her braids. The church ladies would be hosting a social tonight, in their ongoing efforts to keep the male population away from the saloons and certain damnation. There would be music and dancing, all carefully chaperoned by the matrons.

It might be the last one she could make it to before winter sealed her tight in her home. In the interest of flash-fire protection, the mill was at the edge of town. Once the snow drifted, it was safer to stay at home rather than risk the walk through the weather. She'd spend the winter months working the black cast-iron sewing machine that was pushed into the corner of her kitchen. A neat stack of fabric lay waiting for her to cut it into new garments and the scraps would be used for quilt blocks to cover her rough wool blankets and make them comfy. Only the tiniest bits would be tossed into the stove. The idea of hearing music was suddenly tempting beyond her control. She'd be alone with herself soon enough when the weather turned foul.

She wouldn't mind. It was quiet and simple. Today as she sank back into her tub, it was serene. She felt a tiny bit mischievous, completely naked with nothing but water on her skin. There was one more thing for the good matrons in town to berate her for...bathing in the nude. Polite society dictated that young ladies wore a bathing chemise while attending to the chore of cleaning their skin. Blah. That made no sense at all. Once the thin cotton was wet, you could see right through it anyway and she just couldn't justify spending money on a garment that was only used to promote her modesty. The body needed cleaning like everything else in life. She figured the Lord understood, since he'd made her. If she were in some grand school for young ladies, she might need to bathe in a chemise, but not alone on a patch of California homesteaded land.

Moving the soap over her skin raised gooseflesh and sent heat through her belly. Her nipples were hard little peaks that didn't have anything to do with the temperature. No, she was still seeing Sloan's obsidian eyes and the way his gaze had lingered over her body for just the briefest of moments. It was like he'd touched her, stroked every inch of her body and sent heat racing through her blood.

Foolishness? Quite possibly. But the pleasure spreading through her body fascinated her. At twenty, a part of her was actually relieved to discover even base lust moving along her body. Most of the town girls married up by eighteen. There had never been a single man who had made her take a second look at him.

Except Sloan.

Brianna frowned. Too bad he was such a brute. Oh yes, she had seen his type before. The men who laid down their law on anyone and everyone, but most especially their wives. That was, when they married. Few of them did. More than one woman had climbed into the daily stagecoach with disgrace clinging to her hem because of a lawman in town. They were hard men who lived life just as bluntly. Everything was done to the extreme and there was no such thing as flirting with them. They took your hand and didn't stop. It was the one thing her father had insisted she do—steer clear of the rougher element.

Which meant leaving her fantasies of Sloan behind, like her used bath water. It wouldn't be so hard, just stand up and step away from the rush of sensation running over her skin. Reach back and wrap her fingers around the chain that was attached to the plug in the bottom of the tub and give it a yank. The water would run out the drainpipe and flow down the river.

A whole lot like the way Sloan McAlister would climb onto a train and disappear over the ridge one day soon.

Only a fool would lay her body down for a man who wouldn't sleep beside her once he'd had her.

CR

"Miss Spencer."

Gregory Blanery didn't say anything further, but his gaze was fastened onto her through the thick black bars set between his customer and himself. Brianna savored the moment, her best bonnet tied into a careful bow at her chin, along with her best dress. The entire way into town she had been a bundle of tension, her imagination running wild with ideas of bandits stealing her land mortgage money in those moments that it took her to get to the bank. But the last rays of sunlight were fading as she flashed the banker a sweet smile before stepping forward to place her stack of carefully counted money in front of him. His attention instantly focused on the bills, his boney fingers closing around the paper. He counted it faster than she could have, flipping through the bills twice.

"I do believe that settles our account for the next year."

He glared at her for a long second before nodding his head. "It does."

Disappointment laced his words, but it was music to her ears. There would be no land auction to line his pockets. The land note was not even half the value of her father's mill. But if the bank note went into foreclosure, the banker could take everything she couldn't carry away. That would include the heavy grinding stones.

The banker scratched out a receipt and slid it across his counter to her eager hand.

"Until next season."

He grunted at her, but nothing could tarnish her happiness as she tucked the little payment slip into her purse. It was better than money. Stepping outside she paused for a moment to clutch her handbag tight against her chest.

"See, Daddy? I didn't let you down."

Music drifted up from the church as the sun faded completely. Climbing up onto her horse, she rode the short distance to the light spilling out of the church doors. Several teams stood in the cooling night air as their owners flocked inside to share the music. Her step was light as she cast blankets over her horse and went to join them. It was time to celebrate.

He shouldn't touch her.

That thought didn't stick. Sloan wasn't sure it even left a trail as it slipped right out of his brain to make room for the hunger that was doubling in size as he watch Brianna work the last of her coat buttons. A smile touched his lips at the innocent picture she made in the coatroom—she was still wearing her gloves and her fingers were clumsy on the buttons due to the fabric coating her fingers. A silvery giggle escaped her lips as she stopped and tugged her gloves off before stuffing them into a coat pocket. Music floated in on the wind as the light flickered over her smile. She was humming with the fiddle as she shrugged out of her jacket and turned around to place it on a hook.

Brianna had to rise up onto her toes to reach a free hook. The walls already strained under the number of coats and shawls hanging there. It didn't bother her. In fact, it added to the festive atmosphere. A pair of male hands suddenly appeared over hers and plucked her coat from her. A little gasp escaped her lips as sensation rippled along her skin from the contact of bare fingers against bare fingers. It was such a silly thing to notice so intently, but little goose bumps spread along her arms.

Her coat landed on a hook that was sure a whole lot easier for Sloan McAlister to reach with his towering height. Brianna wasn't even certain her head came to the man's shoulders. She turned around and discovered it didn't. Her breath got stuck in her throat as she tipped her chin up to look at his face. It was strange the way her body quivered. On some level, she actually recognized what his skin smelled like and something in her belly jumped at that scent. There was no room to retreat among the coats and wraps. Trapping her, once more close to his frame. The level of awareness she had developed for him was astounding. She felt drawn to him even as her common sense warned her to run.

"Thank you. Guess I should be on time if I want to hang up my coat."

Brianna stared at the way he looked at her. It was an odd detail and her brain insisted on noticing his gaze on her mouth. A shiver raced up her arms, shaking her body hard enough for Sloan to see in the poor light. One corner of his mouth rose slightly as his hand brushed her cheek. The skin-to-skin contact felt so good it was almost exciting. Sloan stepped closer and her foot moved back. The coats wouldn't let her retreat any farther though, forming a soft mountain of fabric that pressed her towards Sloan. His hand moved to her lips where he traced them with his thumb.

Brianna gasped as sensation surged through her. She had no idea her skin could be so aware of a single touch. Her heart raced beneath her corset and her increased respiration drew the warm scent of Sloan's skin deep into her lungs. She'd never imagine that she might like the way any human smelled but tonight, she enjoyed the scent of warm male skin that came with Sloan.

"You're standing under the mistletoe."

She lifted her eyes to look for the little green plant and Sloan leaned down to kiss her. She gasped as he slipped an arm around her to hold her in place. Her hands landed on the wide chest that had tempted her since last night. Each fingertip was alive with awareness as he took command of her mouth.

Who could have explained to her that a man's kiss might burn? Brianna twisted as Sloan's mouth pressed her lips farther apart and the tip of his tongue gently moved over her lower lip. He didn't rush the kiss. It was slow and firm, pressing her mouth open by small, steady degrees. She felt the brush of his fingers along the bare nape of her neck as he gently gripped the tender area, tipping her head back to offer her mouth more fully to his. Heat surged through her blood, igniting a need to get even closer to his body. Her fingertips lamented the fabric preventing her from touching him. A deep groan shook his chest before his tongue thrust into her mouth, breeding an answering whimper from her. His tongue stroked hers and pleasure swirled around her brain so thick, thinking was impossible. Brianna was more interested in lifting her tongue to join the dance and Sloan didn't disappoint her. His tongue twisted with hers as he held her neck in place with that large hand.

A moment later she was free. Sloan stood looking at her with a dark hunger flickering in his eyes. Brianna stared at that emotion as she tried to force her mind to tell her what it was. Her body seemed to understand. Her belly was twisting and her blood racing, but she couldn't quite form a word to describe the flood of sensations that look brought on. Only one thing she knew for certain: she wanted Sloan to kiss her some more.

And she wanted to kiss him back.

That truth frightened her. She knew so little about this man, yet her body was ready, even eager, to offer up her chastity to him. Brianna lifted a hand to cover her mouth as she stared at the hard desire displayed on his face. Sloan was watching, waiting to see what she did in response to his liberty-taking. A Christmas kiss beneath the mistletoe was a quick press of lips. Not the hungry, ravishing embrace he'd just stolen that burned through her senses. Her mouth tingled, sparking a hunger that she was quite at a loss as to how to deal with.

She should slap him or find some sharp, insulting comment to lay on his ears for his boldness. Berate him for acting like a cad. But the thing that kept her staring in stunned silence was the fact that she'd enjoyed it. Her body was saying yes and Brianna wasn't a hypocrite, even if she was weak enough to like his kiss. Heat flowed through her like a river. Insane ideas danced across her imagination, tempting her to reach for him and press her own kiss against his mouth. Return his boldness, measure for measure. It wasn't a ladylike notion at all.

Oh, her mother had certainly tried to teach her better, but the heat bleeding across every inch of her skin only proved Brianna was an extremely poor student.

"It's November. Not Christmas."

Sloan nodded as he gripped his belt. "So it is."

He didn't sound repentant, not one bit. Most men would at least offer an apology for stealing such a kiss right in the church entryway. "Told you not to trust any man. I wanted to kiss you, so I did it. The rules don't really matter when I know how to get around them."

"Kissing me was meant as some kind of warning?"

He jerked slightly, and gripped his belt tighter. His gaze moved for a brief moment as he checked either side of them for any approaching company. When his attention was once again centered on her, a warning flared in his dark eyes.

"Kissing you was enjoyable. I liked it so much, you'd better get inside before I forget you're a virgin."

The knuckles on his hands turned white and Brianna shivered. She could see a battle to let her go burning in his dark eyes, like he was arguing against some inner beast to do the right thing and treat her like a lady.

The horrible reality was a part of her didn't want Sloan to win that fight. The light in the hall suddenly lost its beckoning appeal as Brianna fought the desire to let Sloan pull her away into some dark shadow where they could explore the heat their skin created when they were pressed together. Discover what it was like to be stroked along every part of her body that her dress covered. Her thoughts shocked her as much as they excited her. Forcing her mind to return to the sharper edges of reality, she recalled the face of the last female she'd seen leaving town as a fallen woman. There wouldn't be any reprieve from the judgment of the community and Sloan McAlister didn't strike her as the marrying sort.

"You can stop worrying about me, Mr. McAlister. I heard you just fine and I certainly don't need a man kissing me because he feels sorry for my ignorance. I assure you I can get a kiss without making a man feel pity for me."

It might not be the wisest thing that had ever rolled out of her mouth, but she wasn't going to scurry into the church with her tail tucked between her legs. The man bred a need inside her to prove she was strong enough to handle anything. She didn't want him to see her as weak.

His eyes flashed dark warning at her before she lifted her chin and turned her back on him. Her neck tightened as she moved through the entryway, unsure if her boots were going to remain on the floor. She'd tossed her words at him like a challenge. No way was she going to whimper because he'd treated her like a woman.

But the man loved a challenge. She sensed that about him. While taunting him just might be the dumbest thing she'd ever done, the urge to do so had been irresistible.

Brianna turned and left. Sloan had to force his body to stay right there. He wanted to chase her, run her to ground like a hunter did to its prey. Press another kiss onto her lips just because she'd dared him to.

A deep chuckle shook his chest. He enjoyed the way her hips swayed as she disappeared into the church. She might be a lady, but hidden beneath her calico dress was one fine woman. Part of him enjoyed that idea a little too much. A dark need threatened to take control, tempting him with the notion of making sure he was waiting when she emerged from the social gathering.

Hell, he was a beast most of the time. Embracing those instincts kept him alive when he'd buried men who thought their brainpower was the key to being a long-lived railroad agent.

Sloan stepped back into the street. Noise coming from one of the saloons drifted on the wind, promising him a sample of sin if he was willing to walk away from the church. Down there, temptation would rule as long as the whiskey flowed and no one would think about repenting until sunrise. He should take a little walk and ease the swollen cock that was calling out Brianna's name.

Yeah, well, that wasn't what his cock wanted. The idea of lying between any other woman's thighs left a sour taste in his mouth. Sloan turned and moved back towards his bunkhouse. His eyebrows rose slightly as his cock continued to throb for a little brown-haired virgin.

That wouldn't be happening. The sooner he got that thought through his thick skull, the better. Brianna was everything he didn't even have a right to think about. Men like him didn't lie down with sweet innocents like her. But the scent of her hair lingered as Sloan strolled silently thought the night. He was at home in the dark, always had been.

That was the real trouble. Brianna belonged in a well-lit room with music and scented candles. In spite of her brave words, she'd likely scream if he ever took her to his bed and introduced her to the darker delights he craved. Sure, she'd marry up with one of the town dandies strutting their new bowties and dancing in that church tonight. Brianna would do her duty and spread her thighs for a husband, but she would never cling to a man like he was longing for her to press against him.

"That sure wasn't the wisest move I've seen you make." Warren Howell offered his opinion from his position across the alleyway that ran between the church and the mercantile.

Sloan knew it. Ladies were off-limits and always had been. Just why he was craving one tonight didn't make a whole lot of sense. A pair of blue eyes floated past his memory as the taste of her kiss lingered on his mouth. It was the sort of taste that was going to haunt him. One corner of his mouth lifted as Sloan looked at the light spilling out of the church. Well, if he was going to be haunted, a man couldn't ask for a better specter. A deep chuckle rumbled out of his chest as he walked.

"I wasn't thinking."

Warren lifted an eyebrow in response before falling into step beside him. "I noticed that."

Sloan glared at his fellow railroad agent. Warren was his constant companion. They were comrades who backed each other up. There was no such thing as off-duty. Taking off alone was a good way to be found dead with a bullet in your back. One dead agent meant the men on the rail dock were easier to take out. It could take weeks for replacements to arrive. That was, if there were men to be had. A good agent took training and seasoning. Warren and he shared the shadows regularly. Tonight, he found it a little too claustrophobic. Shrugging beneath his duster, Sloan tried to adjust his attitude. He was headed for a night of dreams haunted by a specter in the form of Brianna Spencer.

Naw, specter wasn't the word...it was siren. A beautiful creature luring him closer with her song. If he followed, it would end in his death.

Yup, sweet siren. But a man could still dream even if he had to hold his course steady. Life rarely delivered the visions of perfection that decorated your dreams.

"But I'm thinking now." Sloan looked at his partner. "So, forget you noticed anything. She's a respectable girl." Sloan actually enjoyed the surge of protectiveness that rose inside him.

Warren didn't comment. He slid a long glance at Sloan before returning his eyes to the darker shadows they were getting ready to pass. The wind whipped up the dust as they crossed the center of town. The noise from the church faded as they headed towards the rail yards. The sound of running water replaced every human-made noise.

Sloan stopped before setting a foot on the first plank of the loading dock. A slight shift and he looked back at the church. Light spilled out through its windows in a display of yellow beams. It was almost mesmerizing to a man who lived his life protecting the sort of law that allowed a haven like the church to exist in a border town. Agents like him and Warren backed up order with hard, cold steel. It had been a long time since he'd noticed the lack of payback for his efforts. Brianna's kiss lingered in his thoughts, a stolen taste of what he devoted his life to protecting. In spite of the fact that he never got to enjoy the haven his efforts produced.

But he wasn't the first man to be tempted by the society he patrolled. A grin lifted his lips as he turned his back on the church. Temptation was a mean spirit, but she sure was a sight for the tired soul to look at.

∾

"I'm going to snatch me a wife, Pa." Joseph Corners was half-drunk, but he enjoyed whiskey so didn't much care that drinking made his mouth run faster than a spring river. His pa looked up and pushed his hat back so that he could get a good look at his son.

"Don't be bringing the law down on this house, boy."

"The law don't need to know." Joseph took another swig from his bottle and rubbed his swollen cock. "I want Brianna Spencer for my bride and I'm going to snatch her up." He snickered as he fantasized about tossing her into his bed. His cock throbbed some more as he licked his lower lip in anticipation of having her at his command. Her sweet skin would be clean, a whole lot better than a used whore. He'd just bet that her pussy smelled nice too.

"Her daddy ever come back from the hills?"

"Naw. Everyone knows he's dead except her. See, that's the best part, Pa. I get me a wife and after I get it all legal-like, that mill is ours. If we was running that mill, we could get a pocket full of gold out of those dumb farmers."

Greed sparkled in his father's eyes. The cabin was dingy and full of mud from the boots of Joseph and his three brothers. His mother had died two years ago and the woman's work had fallen aside with her passing. His pa looked at the greasy cast-iron skillet sitting on the stove.

"Well, I think it might be nice to have a woman around here again. About time one of you boys married up and saw to the keeping of your pa. What's you planning to do, boy? Beat her into submission?"

A hint of enjoyment rushed through him but he shrugged it off. He didn't want to blacken Brianna's face like his pa had done to his ma. There were other ways to control a woman. "Naw, she's a pretty thing."

"But she ain't agreed to marry you. She's got to agree in front of the parson or we don't get the mill." His pa's voice was edgy. Like he was thinking of laying his fist across Joseph's head for not agreeing to beat Brianna into compliance. Sitting up, Joseph wiped his mouth down his sleeve before trying to convince his sire of his plan. He did it fast because his pa wasn't known for his patience and he knew what the older man's fist felt like.

"See, I was thinking. I snatch her up here and lock her away from the rest of the town for the winter. Won't no one really notice once the snow sets in. Remember what you taught me about breaking a mare? I see it sort of like the same thing. If Brianna is forced to depend on me for food, she'll soften up towards me. Get to liking me soon enough, cause I'm all she's got."

"Not too bad an idea, son."

Joseph grinned because his pa only called him son when he was proud of him. "Besides, I figure if we got's us a baby on the way, Brianna will be in a fine hurry to marry me before her belly gets too big."

His pa snickered. "Well now, it can get mighty cold up here in the winter. Seems like you'd better plan on keeping that pretty little girl warm."

Joseph snatched up his whiskey bottle and offered it to his pa. The older man took a swig before passing it back. Joseph rubbed his cock again and grinned as he considered just how to place his plan into action. With his pa on his side, his brothers wouldn't be no trouble. In fact, they'd help out, considering there was a woman's cooking to be gained.

He didn't doubt he'd have Brianna stoking the dirty black stove in front of him. She'd bend to his command just like a prairie pony did when you starved it long enough. He licked his lower lip as he considered what she might do when her belly ached bad enough for food. Some of them whores did some mighty fine things with a man's cock. Seeing as how Brianna had all the same parts as those women, he was looking forward to having her at his mercy. Planting a baby in her belly wasn't going to be half the fun, not hardly.

Chapter Three

Brianna awoke to discover that winter wasn't wasting any time in arriving. There was ice on the river this morning. Small clumps of snow lay on the bank and they didn't completely melt away by afternoon. Ice flowed down the river, heralding the onslaught of the cold weather.

Brianna ran a longing hand over a new length of flannel fabric waiting near her sewing machine. Making a winter dress sounded wonderful. She stroked the black cast-iron machine with a loving finger, taking a moment to enjoy the fact that she didn't have to sew by hand anymore. Powered by a foot treadle, the sewing machine practically flew through stitching fabric together. Every stitch was perfect too. Just watching it made her giddy like a child with a new toy. Only it was a woman's toy. Her father had bought the machine last season and she still had trouble believing she owned such a modern convenience. It sure would save money, if she could make her own clothing instead of buying garments at the mercantile.

More money might even be earned if she made men's shirts and sold them in town. Home goods went for a good sum in Silver Peak due to the lack of women. Miners wore out their shirts and without a wife they were reduced to buying new ones from women who had learned how to make money with housewifery skill. More than one westerner found himself being kept by his wife, when his dreams of striking gold didn't materialize. Savvy women had discovered that their skills in the home were worth cash to the hordes of miners. Once her daddy returned, she might just take up tailoring and strike a bargain with the mercantile in town.

With two incomes, the land bill wouldn't be a problem ever again. A bright smile covered her face as she gave the machine a loving pat. Yes sir, she and her father were going to make it in the West without finding any gold. They would just provide the services that the miners and farmers needed. Back east, huge factories kept a single family from prospering. That was why her father had moved them west. Opportunity was here for those bold enough to pit their fortunes against the harshness of getting started.

The creaking of a wagon interrupted her ideas. She went to the door to peek out of the view hole now that her window was boarded closed.

A smile moved her lips up as the widow Lambert climbed down from her buckboard. Bonnie Lambert was as sweet as a summer strawberry. Pushing the bar up, Brianna pulled the door open and stepped into the yard to greet her guest. Bonnie wouldn't have any money to offer, but she always waited until the end of the season before attempting to barter for her grinding. That sort of consideration made her a good friend. The widow had lost her husband to fever after an accident, but her three young sons still managed to bring in enough of a crop to feed the family. Brianna would bet the widow had been sending her youngest son over the hill to look at the river every morning this week to see if the ice was getting thicker. Judging the perfect time to make her appearance.

"Good afternoon, Bonnie. Is that Tomas? How did he get so tall?"

CR

Brianna worked into dusk on the Lambert grain. It was actually less expensive to burn kerosene in her lamps for work light than coal in her stove to heat the cabin. The labor of working the mill kept her warm, so she lit the lamp. It was a race against winter, because her mill used water to power it. Once the river iced over three feet from the banks, there would be no more grinding until spring. She couldn't risk breaking the waterwheel that powered the grinding stone.

That was a shame, too. She had enough work to grind all winter, but you couldn't hold back ice. She had begun turning farmers away weeks ago. They would bring their grain back once spring arrived, because she couldn't be responsible for their crops during the winter. Every order she took now would be on a day-to-day basis. She had no way to judge just when the cold would force her to stop. It was something she would have to decide each morning.

Staying up past sunset was the only way to ensure she finished the order. The early morning hours might bring ice that ended her grinding. Besides, the Lambert family only needed their personal flour and cornmeal ground. Bonnie needed to feed her family. Brianna grinned as she stretched out her back. It was worth the ache in her spine. Bonnie had milk cows and she had brought sweet butter to trade. Placed in the back bedroom, it would freeze and keep all the way into spring once Brianna spooned it into thick crocks. The idea of hot biscuits with butter kept her company as she worked into the evening.

She only walked up to her cabin to light another lamp so that she wouldn't have to stumble around in a pitch-black room. Now that the window was nailed shut, the front room was dim even during daylight. Checking the lamp, she turned the wick down as far as possible and made sure the lamp was only a third full of oil. She sat the glass lamp in her large cast-iron cooking pot as a precaution against fire. If it turned over, the fire would be contained in the deep iron pot.

Rubbing her arms, she left the cabin and hurried back to the mill house. A single lamp was lit near the grinding stone and it welcomed her with its yellow glow. Pushing the door closed against the night chill, she clasped the handle that would lower the grinding stone onto the grain waiting to be crushed by its weight. She was going to splurge and make herself an over jacket with that sewing machine. A nice, thick wool one that she could button over her bodice and stays to keep her warm. With the speed of the sewing machine, she'd have the time to make one instead of struggling to keep up with replacing the garments that had worn out past spring and summer.

"Shut up, dumb ass. She'll hear you."

Brianna froze as the words floated in the open mill house window. She hadn't dared nail this window shut. The air would become a thick, swirling mass of chafe and grain partials if she didn't let the wind in. Turning the wick down on her lamp, she moved across the floor to peer into the darkness that surrounded her cabin. A horrified gasp left her lips as she watched the dark shapes of men in the night. There was a smack and the splintering sound of a wall being torn apart on her cabin. Backing up, she looked around the mill house, cursing her lack of foresight in leaving her father's rifle up in the cabin. All of her pride shattered as she recognized the pure reality of how helpless she was in the face of lawless men. She had no idea who was breaking into her home or what they wanted, but might made right as darkness masked their deeds. The sound of more wood being splintered sent her franticly searching for any means of protection.

The horses belonging to her invaders were still in the main drive. One false move and they'd tell their masters that she was scurrying away towards town. The mill house door opened onto that drive and might spook the team if she tried to escape the mill. Chewing on her lip, she considered the only other way out. A trapdoor was set into the floor. It was there for cleaning. You just swept everything out the hatch. Many times she'd washed the plank floor down with buckets of water because she could push the water right out of the room through the trapdoor.

But there was nothing on the banks of the river to hide behind. Leaving the mill house would get her out of sight of her midnight bandits, but it wouldn't be much of a trade-off. The only escape the hatch offered her was a freezing cold river that just might kill her faster than the men breaking into her home.

"The bitch ain't here. Try the mill."

Freezing water or not, she wasn't waiting for them to check the mill house. Slipping through the open trapdoor, Brianna pressed the hatch back into place once she was crouched beneath the mill. The mud was frozen and her boots slipped on the ice. Heavy boots came down the drive as she turned and slid across the ice on the banks of the river. Her body went right into the flowing center of the water.

She gasped as she plunged into the near-freezing liquid. Needles pricked up and down her limbs as the current carried her downstream. Moving her arms, she tried to swim faster towards town. Sure, people claimed that death was preferable to dishonor, but she wanted to live. Not end up a victim of the icy current. Keeping her head above the water became harder as her body lost more heat. She could feel the ice on her lips as she gasped for breath and strained to keep her neck up out of the swirling, freezing tempest. The river was trying to pull her into its center. She fought to get back to the slower-moving water along the banks, but ice was thick there and her fingers slipped off every time she tried to grip it.

Gasping for another breath, she watched the hazy glow of light penetrate the cold trying to numb her brain. The image danced in a crazy motion, with rays shooting out like a star. Forcing her body to strain towards it took every last shred of will that she had. A harsh cry left her lips as she pushed forward, grasping at that single promise of life.

Pain exploded along her shoulder as she smacked into one of the support beams that made up the dock. All the force of the current went into her, racking her with pain, but she clamped her arms around the rough wood refusing to let loose of the only possibility of escape from the river. Hard shivers shook her as she tried to move her hand farther up the beam to begin climbing out of the river. Her limbs shook violently, but refused to do as her brain commanded. Gritting her teeth, she grunted and forced her hands to claw at the slick wood, welcoming the pain from countless splinters because it meant she was still alive. A dark haze beckoned to her from the water rushing past. It pulled at her dress, clutching at her petticoat, attempting to drag her back into the current. Almost a promise of release from the pain, but she refused to sink into its welcoming folds.

Because life hurt.

She knew it. Faced it each and every day, and she wanted to confront it again. Not slip back into the river and the cold, unfeeling embrace of death. Digging her fingers into the wood, she cried as it ripped her skin again, but she pulled her shoulders out of the water in spite of the pain.

"Jesus Christ!"

Her entire body was hauled out of the water in one swift moment. She flopped onto the dock as her legs collapsed. She contorted in a violent attack of shivering unable to do anything but convulse on the rough planks. Her dress and petticoat were soaked. The weight of the wet fabric felt too much to lift as her heart struggled to move her cold blood. Each breath took an amazing amount of strength to draw into her lungs, every thump of her heart sounded like a gavel landing. Her throat wouldn't let a single word out as she kicked against her wet clothing in a vain attempt to stand. But she wasn't even able to roll onto her hands and knees.

"Holy hell." A hard hand gripped her head and turned her face up to Sloan's. "Look at me." His voice was as hard as his grip. Demand edged the tone as he let her chin go and slipped his hand under the tangled mess of her hair to press flush against her neck. She jolted as the sting cut through the chill moving along her veins. His flesh was as hot as a poker pulled from the fire, sending another rush of agony down her back.

"Don't you dare close your eyes, Brianna."

Her lips wouldn't cooperate enough for her to answer. She couldn't get them to form any words. All that escaped her throat was a jumble of sounds that betrayed how much she hurt. Every patch of flesh was ablaze with pain that slashed deep into her joints. He grasped her wrist and bent his knees. With another yank, Sloan flung her over his shoulder. He straightened up without a second of hesitation and moved across the dock at a brisk pace, his boots making sound because of his hurry. She should have been horrified to have her fanny facing up, but it felt like ice was moving through her and it hurt too much for her to worry about anything else. She tried to grasp the black fabric of his duster, to steady her head, but her hands refused to close into a grip.

A door opened and Sloan kicked it shut behind them. The air in the room burned her cheeks, it felt so warm. She gasped as Sloan let her down. "Try and stand, honey. I've got to get your dress off."

"B-b-but—" Her teeth knocked against one another as Sloan placed his rifle against the wall. He took hold of her shoulders and steadied her.

"It's full of ice." He stroked a hand over her head and through her hair. Ice hit the floor with a rattle that startled her. She looked down in confusion right before she hissed as Sloan's fingers touched her neck.

"You're h-h-ot."

"No, honey, you're cold. The kind of cold that kills." His voice was hard but not angry. He grabbed the top of her dress and opened the first few buttons. Disbelief spread through her as she tried to wiggle away from his touch.

"Your face is blue." He caught her shoulders and held her steady as he locked gazes with her. "A dip in an icy river can stop a man's heart. Your dress needs to come off. Now."

He finished opening the front of her dress as she tried to think. Caught between the horror of dying and the idea of being undressed in front of him, her mind was completely overwhelmed. He slid her open dress right down her torso and over her hips before she mustered a response. She tried to push his hands aside, but her muscles weren't obeying her brain's commands. She still shivered violently, clenching her teeth together to keep them from chattering. Each touch from Sloan's fingers felt hot enough to sear her skin.

"I'm sorry, honey, but I only know one way to warm you back up." His voice was thick with determination. "The clothes come off."

Brianna looked up to stare into his eyes. A second later he grabbed the tie lacing her stays. A hard jerk and she felt the garment begin to slacken. He pulled at the cord until her corset dropped to the floor.

"Oh no..." Her words were whisper soft and full of embarrassment. Her chemise was plastered to her wet skin, leaving very little of her body a mystery. Never once had she ever considered being viewed by a man, even a husband in such a way.

"Body heat is the only way to keep you from dying on me."

The harsh note in his voice frightened her. It was the same tone he'd used on Joseph while aiming his rifle at the man's gut. She wiggled once more but he followed her and hooked his fingers into the shoulders of her last garment. He pulled her chemise right over her head. He gripped her hips, and her knickers, along with her petticoat, went down her legs so fast she wasn't sure when he unbuttoned them. A shower of ice hit the floor, filling the small cabin with a rattling sound. Looking down, she stared at the harsh truth of just how dangerous a situation she was in. Her clothing was frozen. Getting free of it was the only way to warm back up.

But that left her nude.

A little sound of horror escaped her lips as she found herself standing bare in front of a man. Her brain flatly refused to grasp the complete idea of it. Sloan didn't give her any time to consider what he was doing. He scooped her up and moved across the floor. He settled her into his bunk in one efficient motion.

"I'm sorry, honey, but modesty isn't worth your life."

The black duster landed on top of the blankets she was under. He glared at her for a long moment before moving his rifle to lean against the nightstand. He watched her face as he began to open his shirt. She should have protested and found some harsh retort to force past her frozen lips, but she became distracted by the hard flesh each turn of a button revealed. She'd seen her father a few times, bare above the waist, but Sloan looked nothing like her daddy. His chest was wide and covered with thick ridges of muscle. Dark hair ran across his chest, covering each flat male nipple. The dark hair continued down over his belly to disappear under his waistband. He turned and sat on the bunk, levering his boots off. A second later he rolled under the covers and reached for her.

Contact with his flesh hurt. He was too hot and she strained away from him. Sloan pressed her right back against his body. She could feel his heart beating against her breasts as he hugged her firmly against his burning heat.

"We have to get your temperature up to normal."

He smoothed his hands over her back, molding their frames together. His feet and legs joined the embrace, one knee going right between her thighs. She shook violently as his warm skin touched her. Fear surged through her as she recognized just how correct he was. Her swim had placed her far too close to the border of death. The steady throb of his heart against her own suddenly beckoned with the promise of life.

"All right." Her voice was working again. Brianna sighed as she stopped shivering and her muscles began to relax. Tension flowed out of her as she slumped against the solid body heating her frozen flesh. Sloan's hands moved constantly, smoothing over her spine and her head and even down to her hips. The crisp hair covering his chest teased her skin as she nuzzled her nose against his neck to thaw it. She was suddenly more comfortable than she could remember being in a very long time. Her lungs filled and her eyes refused to remain open as she pressed closer to the warm male holding her. There was no more reason to struggle.

She couldn't think and she discovered that she didn't want to. Not while the scent of Sloan's skin filled her senses. She'd get back to contemplating her actions later. For the moment she just wanted to indulge her body and be cradled by his strength while she reaped the benefits of not giving up during her fight to live.

Leaning on him appealed to her as her brain slipped into that dark oblivion it had resisted back in the river.

God was getting even with him. Sloan wanted to cuss, but gritted his teeth instead. He stroked the back of Brianna's head and listened to her breathing even out. Tiny shivers still shook her body as she nuzzled against his neck, and his cock ached.

Yup, the Almighty was calling in a few debts tonight, but it was worth it. Somehow, the privilege of holding her was worth a whole hell of a lot of frustration. Leaning down, he buried his face in her hair and inhaled her sweet scent. It was the purest form of torture, the way her skin smelled. Like roasting meat to a starving man. Time stood still while it worked its way around his head, pushing each and every other thought aside. There was only the craving and the scent that awakened it.

Hell.

He gritted his teeth against the feel of her satin-soft skin. She smelled more feminine than he could recall a female ever doing. Almost like she was clean and pure, better somehow than the last woman who'd shared his bed. Her nipples were twin little points poking into his chest. He had to remind himself that it was an icy river that had raised the tender flesh into peaks. Not her journey into his bed. His cock didn't much care about the detail. The flesh was hard and aching inside his pants, demanding freedom from his britches. He'd left that single garment on, unwilling to trust himself with her clothing lying on the floor. It had been a good bet. There was no way he'd stand the feeling of her thighs against his cock.

"Stay awake, honey."

His endearment roused her. No one called her "honey" and she'd made sure a few of her more base customers understood that respect was a must if they wanted their grain ground. Sweet-talking wasn't going to jump their order to the front of her line or gain them a seat at her supper table. Sloan clasped the back of her neck and tipped her head up so that their eyes met. There wasn't a lot of light in the room, but she felt his stare just about as much as she saw it.

"You go to sleep while you're this cold and you might not wake up."

"Oh…of course." She knew that. When the body was too cold, you had to keep your eyes open. She remembered now. That was why she was fighting to feel the pain back in the river.

But she was so tired! Bone weary and it was too hard to keep her eyelids up. They fluttered as she fought to stay awake, but her strength was gone, completely drained.

"I just need to rest my eyes is all." Her eyelids closed and she sighed in relief.

Sloan cupped her breast and her eyes bulged open. "Sloan McAlister!" Her voice cracked as she felt each one of his fingers grasping her breast, holding the tender globe with a steady grip that didn't squeeze too hard. A gleam of enjoyment entered his eyes as he gently stroked her breast, his thumb grazing the sharp point of her nipple. Sensation flooded her, rushing through her chest and over to the opposite breast.

"Stay awake, Brianna, or I'll be happy to help you."

Heat snaked through her breast, moving across the delicate skin to the hard nipple. Pleasure filled her as she discovered that she enjoyed the way his hand felt on her. It was a terrible time to discover such a fact. Until that moment, her breasts were rarely thought about. The corset lying on the floor kept them laced securely every day. Sloan watched her eyes for a moment before he slid his hand off her tender flesh and down over her ribs. He stroked her back once more as a little wave of disappointment hit her. Her breast missed his touch, the nipple begging for his fingers to stroke it. The idea was so intoxicating she became lost in it, her eyes fluttering shut once more so that she could hide the fantasy from his probing gaze.

He cupped one side of her bottom next. She jumped as his fingers curled around her cheek and right into the space between her legs. Her head cracked against his chin as she bucked away from the unaccustomed touch. A soft grunt hit her ears, but the hand on her fanny tightened, rubbing and kneading the private portion of her body.

"You can't do that." But he was and as hard as she tried to remember just why it wasn't allowed, Brianna couldn't find an answer. All her mind seemed concerned with was the heat moving from where his hand gripped her bottom to that secret part of her body between her thighs. The heat snaked right down the center of her slit to the front where a tiny throbbing began.

"Keep your eyes open and I won't." His voice was gruff and unsteady for the first time that she could recall. She stared at the taut expression on his face, her eyes held wide open by a mixture of shock and excitement.

"That's right, honey."

His hand left after a final squeeze and a little whimper escaped her lips. Surprise flashed across his face as she bit into her lower lip in confusion. Sloan's obsidian gaze dropped to where her teeth were pushing into her lip. Hunger filled his gaze and it sent a surge of heat through her. All ideas of slumber dissipated as she opened her jaw and licked her lower lip instead of biting it.

He cussed, low and deep, before capturing the nape of her neck in one strong hand. He angled his head to fit his mouth against hers. It was a hard kiss but that fit his embrace. Her nipples tingled as he clasped her against his chest. He pushed her lips apart, the tip of his tongue licking over her lower lip. It was vastly different than the feel of her own tongue. His was strong and male. He pressed his kiss harder against her mouth as he rolled her onto her back, her thighs parting as his hips nudged them apart.

Another whimper rose from her throat, but this time it was born somewhere in the pulsing current of heat flowing through her. Her hands reached for his warm skin, stroking over it, absorbing more heat. Her back arched towards his hard chest and she moaned as pleasure went through her breasts pressed against his chest. It felt so perfect, the contact between their bodies. Her breasts were soft and his chest was hard—they complemented each other.

"Jesus, Brianna. I didn't mean to drag you into this." His voice was gruff in that way that you apologized for something you knew was wrong, but you liked enough to shoulder the shame.

She didn't want to stop, didn't want Sloan to think about anything but kissing her some more. Lifting her head she tried to press her mouth against his, but his fingers on her neck held her in place.

"No, honey. I'm a hell of a lot of things, but I'm not a bastard who'll take your body when you didn't land in my bed under your own choice."

God knew he wanted to take her. Sloan growled as he pressed her flat onto her back. Everything inside him agreed with the sight of her beneath him, but the memory of the spunk in her eyes held him away from what he wanted to take from her. That surge of protectiveness surfaced above his lust and he soaked up its soothing presence. Being worthy of her was more important than fucking her because he could. It was a subtle moment as he balanced on the edge of giving in to the instinct to just take and instead grasped the opportunity to prove that he could do the correct thing by leaving her chaste.

Men could choose to not act like animals. That was what defined you as a decent man opposed to the lawless scum sharing the earth with you. Some men were better than others. They earned respect through perseverance.

But he wasn't going to leave her wanting either.

Moving a hand over her body, he locked her down as his opposite hand smoothed across her belly to her spread thighs. She jerked as passion battled against her morals but the scent of her arousal hit his senses, confirming that he wasn't alone in his cravings.

She moaned. Deep and low, like some animal. Brianna was shocked by her own sound as Sloan touched the most intimate part of her body. Heat poured through her as he stroked a single finger through her folds. Her flesh was slick for some reason and sweet sensation spiked up into her belly as he fingered her again. He stopped at the top of her sex, rubbing gently over a hard button hidden there.

"You can't touch me...like that." Her voice, breathless and husky, stunned her with just how carnal she sounded.

He leaned down until she felt his breath against her moist lips. "You enjoy it, don't you?"

He stroked her again as she gasped. Pleasure shook her as her hips bucked beneath his hand. He pressed her flat onto his bed as he rubbed faster. Her lungs couldn't seem to keep up with her heart as sweat popped out on her skin.

"Sloan..."

He kissed her to end her comment. His finger rubbed her and a moment later pleasure exploded under his touch. She screamed because it was just too much to keep inside her body. Such an abundance of sensation. It snapped her body like a leather whip. His mouth absorbed her cries as he slowly stroked her slit a few final times. Gently now, only a smooth touch of his fingers against that bud at the top of her slit.

"Now you can go to sleep, honey."

Her breath was slowing down as she tried to lift her eyelids and demand...something...from him. But her brain refused to be denied the sweet slumber it had been looking for since her struggle to live began. Her body was full of little ripples of delight and they rocked her like a babe. Sloan smoothed and cradled her body, pushing her into sleep as contentedly as a child now that she was warm, the fingertips resting on his chest no longer icy.

He felt the steady beat of her heart as he hugged her close. If there had ever been a single moment in his life that might be termed perfect, this was it.

Yeah, he was a bastard but he wasn't a defiler. When Brianna spread her body for his use, she would do it with full surrender or he would take his cock to bed hard. His life was often harsh and brutal, but at the center of everything that he was, Sloan still had his principles.

He wanted her and that meant all of her. Complete surrender or nothing at all.

It wasn't something he needed to rush. Guilt weighed on his conscience as he looked at her dress lying in a wet puddle on the floor. Little shivers still shook her body, and he hugged her closer as she continued to relax and let the tension leave her mind. His temper heated up faster. There weren't many reasons that would have sent her into the river. None of them were good. She was restless, wiggling and kicking against his embrace. Whatever had frightened her bad enough to go swimming still rattled around in her brain. Smoothing a hand over her wet hair, he felt his resolve harden. Sure, it wasn't his job, maybe not even his business, but he was going to uncover just who had driven Brianna into an icy current. Whatever—or whoever—she'd been trying to escape needed killing.

He was just the man for the job. That was one place he did belong. Enforcing the law. Brianna shouldn't have to face that ugly reality of life. It wasn't his job to enforce civility on the culprit, but at that moment, with her head resting on his shoulder, he was tempted to make it his responsibility. It sure felt personal. Sloan smiled at the idea and let it rest in his mind for a bit. Temptation was one of those things that he just couldn't keep himself from considering once in a while.

Tonight, it was sleeping in his bed.

And no one took what was his. Even if he hadn't taken it himself.

Chapter Four

Brianna stretched her legs and sighed. She felt as content as a cat. The bed was warm and there was plenty of room for her toes. Even the air on her face was cozy. Her eyelashes fluttered while her brain attempted to clear the night's slumber from it. If the room was warm, she'd put too much coal in the stove. That was an oversight her budget couldn't afford.

She tried to push herself up, but the blankets keeping her so toasty-warm held her to the bed. Kicking at the stubborn bedding, she dislodged a corner and sat up. Her eyes rounded with horror as she cast a look around the cabin. Unfamiliar and Spartan, furnished with the bare basics. A black cast-iron stove sat in the corner, a small pot-bellied model. A neat cupboard stood next to it with a few tins stored on the upper shelves. Heat radiated from the stove and her dress was draped over the back of a chair sitting a few feet in front of it.

Her face burned scarlet as she looked down at her nude body. There was nothing on her but what she'd come into the world wearing—skin. She was caught between the need to giggle and groan, because not once in her memory could she recall being bare for an entire night. A part of her found it ridiculously amusing, just as long as she didn't look too closely at the fact that it had really happened.

And Sloan McAlister had stripped her down...

Tossing the blankets off, she hurried across the wooden floor to snatch her knickers off the seat of the chair. There was no sign of her shoes, making her hiss in anger as she realized the harsh current must have plucked her footwear right off her feet. She could add a pair of shoes to whatever else had been stolen from her house last night. The moment she closed her grip around her knickers, pain burned up her arms. Dropping her knickers she looked at her hands. Dark splinters decorated her palms and fingers. The skin had swelled up around the little daggers. Clinging to dock last night hadn't been without its price. However she was still breathing, so she welcomed the little shards of wood as a testimony to her will to survive.

The possibility of being completely wiped out, right down to her shoes was too frustrating to contemplate. Better to wait until she was staring at the burned-out shell of her father's mill before thinking the worst. Hope might not be much, but it sure beat desolation. At least the grinding stone couldn't burn. The waterwheel that powered it was another matter too grim to entertain until she was forced to. Replacing that would mean taking out a second mortgage against the land note to pay a carpenter. That would saddle her with two notes to pay and only her to earn money. It was a vicious circle. She couldn't mill without a waterwheel and she couldn't build one herself.

The stove was glowing with heat, but gooseflesh raced along her limbs as she picked her knickers back up. Shimmying into the garment, she ignored the complaint from her splinters long enough to cover her nudity. Her face turned red as she contemplated facing Sloan, but at least she would do it with her dress buttoned!

Never mind that he knew exactly what she looked like and felt like beneath the worn calico. Her nipples tingled as her mind offered up a crystal clear recollection of the burst of pleasure he'd unleashed in her last night.

"Oh, Brianna Spencer, you're a shame."

Working the busk on the front of her corset, she kept glancing at the door. Turning, she placed her back towards it as she stepped into her petticoat. Wiggling her hips, she sent its hem towards her feet. The cotton was completely dry and felt cozy against her legs. After she'd fallen asleep, Sloan must have remained awake and hung her wet garments up. Her face remained hot as she pushed her arms into her dress sleeves. In spite of being innocent, she wasn't ignorant as to just why Sloan hadn't drifted off into slumber as she had.

He hadn't been satisfied.

Her mother's ghost was going to rise up and haunt her. Brianna felt the icy grip of moral retaliation grazing her shoulder as she looked around for something to brush her hair with. It was a tangled mess, half of her hairpins long gone. She picked out the remaining ones when she found a small mirror on the opposite side of the room. A large comb sat beside the porcelain basin beneath it. A thick length of leather hung on the wall as well as a razor. A shiver went down her spine as she gazed at the masculine items. There was something intimate about being in his private space. Certainly, she had toyed with the idea of marrying and sharing a home with a man, but that hadn't prepared her for the pure rush of sensation that moved through her right then. A hint of vulnerability touched her body as she realized just how easy it was for Sloan to handle her. The surge of enjoyment that went along with it all confused her. As if a part of her liked being bent to a man's will. It didn't make much sense. But there was no denying she liked it. Lying to herself wouldn't change the facts.

She didn't understand just what he'd managed to draw from her body last night. Another ripple of sensation moved over her, but this time it was deeper and shot down her spine to that spot between her thighs that he'd touched. She had never been much of a gossip, but a few rumors had made their way past her ears. She'd heard that some women enjoyed their marriages more than others. It didn't make any sense and, somehow, she hadn't felt comfortable asking her father about it. It seemed more like a question a daughter took to her mother. Maybe because only a woman knew a female's body.

Well, Sloan sure did know a thing or two as well...

Pulling the comb down the length of her hair, she looked in the mirror at the blush staining her face. The memory of last night was bright as the noon sun. It shimmered with all the sensation that had raced through her flesh, twisting and tightening under his touch, making her wonder this morning at just how much more intense it might be if she yielded completely. Cross that boundary into womanhood by allowing Sloan to find his own comfort deep inside her body.

Oh, she knew the blunt facts concerning procreation, but she understood very little about the reason why men craved the act so much. From what she'd seen, not all men liked the babies that arrived nine months after they got the favors of their ladyloves. Silver Peak was full of miners who lamented the hard work needed to fill their children's bellies. But that didn't stop them from kissing those same women out behind the feed store when they thought no one was looking.

Some women craved the pleasures of the flesh, too. The good mothers at the church socials called them "fallen women". But just what was it about enjoying your own body that was wrong? Sloan had sent delight streaming through her with just his hands, and if that was dirty, she didn't really understand why.

Well, she'd have plenty of time to contemplate it after seeing to the matter of her home.

After pinning her hair up as best she could, Brianna turned to the bed. She shook out the bedding and tucked it neatly on top of the bunk. Once she'd replaced the chair against the wall, it was impossible to tell she had ever been in the room. A naughty little smile covered her lips briefly as she considered the dark hours that she had lain with Sloan. She pressed the secret against her heart for a moment of stolen enjoyment before turning towards the door. Reality was waiting and the consequences of being lazy were never kind. She had to take stock of the damage and decide how to face the winter without starving. The only bright point was the sure knowledge that she had taken Clayton's money to the bank. Having applied it to the mortgage on her father's property, she didn't need to fear the banker until spring. That left her facing the weather. Better odds, but still a challenge.

Hesitating, she looked over the belongings near the basin. A leather case caught her eye and she deliberated opening it to find some tweezers to pull her splinters. She rolled her eyes at her own bashfulness and lifted the male grooming kit off the wooden side table. A razor and lather brush was neatly stored inside it, along with trimming scissors and a pair of silver tweezers. Pulling them free, she held her hand up to the morning sunlight to begin removing the shreds of wood. Tears stung her eyes as she picked at the deeper ones, but she still was happy to feel the pain. She finished up the chore by washing her hands with soap and water to clean the wounds. They stung as the lather covered them. An unladylike grunt filled the cabin as she replaced the tool.

Pushing the bar up, she opened the door. Icy cold bit at her cheeks. Instead of sunlight, there was only the gray light of a day promising a storm. Her foot halted one step from the threshold. Another dark-eyed man watched her from three feet in front of the door. Her hand froze on the handle as she stared into his serious expression. Whoever the man was, his eyes studied her for a long moment before he offered her a slight nod. He touched the brim of his dark felt Stetson.

"Morning, ma'am." He returned his hand to the revolver sitting on an overturned section of a tree in front of him. His fingers moved in slow motions over the weapon, polishing it. "Warren Howell, at your service."

His voice was steady and smooth, just like the motion of his hands over the barrel of his gun. A rifle was propped up against his knee within easy reach. His gaze shifted around the dock briefly before returning to her. "You'll want to step back inside."

Brianna swallowed the lump in her throat. There was no point in getting twisted up in some idea of what others thought of her. She knew the facts concerning just how she'd landed in Sloan's boarding room. As well as the knowledge that she wasn't missing anything a future husband might expect her to have on their wedding night. "Excuse me, but I will be on my way."

Forcing her frozen feet forward, she moved forward into the light of day and pressed the door closed behind her. There was a faint rustle of fabric as Warren Howell stood. He stepped right over the tree section he was using as a table and she had to tip her head back to look at his face.

"You'll need to step back inside, ma'am." Solid authority rang in his deep tone. Although his words were the model of perfect manners, it wasn't a request any longer. Hard determination flickered in his gaze. His eyes were a strange combination of colors that reminded her of whiskey. "Sloan will explain things to you as soon as he concludes his business. He left me to look after you until then."

A ripple of excitement went through her, but right after that her pride flared up in response to being left under guard. Maybe Sloan McAlister was accustomed to laying down orders, but she wasn't bound to obey him.

Not that you minded it last night, missy...

Her curiosity was going to land her in a mess of trouble if she listened to it. She was leaving and promptly too. "Thank you for your concern, Mr. Howell, but I have work to attend to."

She had made it two paces from the front door before Warren hooked her arm and spun her in a circle back to where she'd begun. He did it expertly and with a solid control that made her gasp. The man was every inch as deadly as Sloan, but she wasn't aware of him in the same heated way. She stared at him for a long moment as she tried to reason out just why he didn't strike her the same way Sloan did. His features were smoother and more handsome than Sloan's, but she still didn't feel that twist in her lower belly. There was no rising heat in her face, only a flicker from her temper at being thought easy to intimidate.

"My apologies, sir, but you will have to extend my regrets to Mr. McAlister." She used her firmest voice and kept her back straight with her chin steady, but Warren wasn't impressed.

"No, ma'am. You'll have to take the matter up with him yourself. But you will be here when he returns." There was a chink of chain as Warren reached behind his back and drew a pair of handcuffs off his belt. Her mouth actually dropped open as she viewed his threat. She blinked a few times as disbelief stunned her. But the iron bracelets didn't vanish and the stern look on Warren's face told her the man was dead serious.

"You are quite out of line, sir."

"That may be, ma'am, but you're not walking off on my watch." The hint of concern in his deep voice perplexed her. Any manner of empathy seemed completely misplaced when the man threatened her with physical restraint. "Now, turn around and go cook up some breakfast for yourself. You'll find that a hard task with one of these iron bracelets on your arm." He moved the handcuffs and the metal rattled against itself, making her flinch. Her hands clasped behind her back in an unconscious defensive motion. Warren took one long step closer.

"But you are staying put until Sloan returns from checking out your place. That's man's work and I gave him my word that you'd be here when he got done making sure your unwelcome guests didn't just bed down when they found the place empty. Don't worry, he didn't go alone." Warren softened his voice a tad with his last statement. A clear effort to ease his order, but the look in his eyes wasn't softening one bit. "Now don't make me lock up a pretty lady like yourself. Step back inside."

Her gaze darted from side to side as she tried to conceive a plan of escape. Her ears detected a soft hiss of male disgruntlement before her upper arm was hooked. Warren's grip was firm and unyielding as he turned her around. He pulled the wooden door open and pushed her through the doorway before she swallowed the unladylike retort she wanted to fling at him.

"One step out and I'll chain you to that bunk...ma'am. Lady or not."

The "ma'am" was added on as an afterthought. Brianna turned and watched the door being closed. A blast of air hit her face because she was standing so close when it was stopped by the doorjamb. The wood actually touched the hem of her skirt.

Her temper caught fire as she snarled at the rough wood panel. She stomped beneath her petticoat, but she couldn't do a whole lot. Sure, it wasn't legal, but she would have to complain to the sheriff in order to get anything done about it. That meant getting out of her impromptu prison. Pulling the door open, she looked straight into Warren's somber expression. He was right back in his seat facing the door. One of his dark eyebrows rose as she looked at him over the tree stump. He stretched his tall frame up out of his seat and flexed his hands.

"Brute."

"Ma'am." With a little snort, she let the door fall closed against the challenge written on his face. Pacing her way around the room she tried to bring some kind of order to her thoughts. Being mad only sent her rational thinking up in smoke. Gaining a grip on her emotions was the key to thinking her dilemma through.

But her temper sure didn't agree.

Her belly rumbled but she didn't stop pacing to cook. Stoking up the fire in the stove felt like hoisting a white flag. She wasn't surrendering to Sloan's will. Not Brianna Spencer. She'd made it just fine without a man and today wasn't going to be the moment she cried like a little lost girl just because life had decided to turn tough. She was made of sterner stuff.

But Sloan didn't think so. That thought deflated her completely. It actually humbled her, because it had been a long time since she'd encountered a man who made someone else's troubles his own. Even a good number of sheriffs needed a nudge to look into things. They often had friends who took precedence over the written law of the state. If your dispute was on the wrong side of those friendship lines, you might just find yourself waiting a long time for any lawman to investigate an incident. But some mining towns were far worse off. At least they had a sheriff who hadn't bought his badge or, worse yet, been placed in his office by the saloon owners. The fledgling state was rife with loose concepts of just what United States law was.

That brought in men like Sloan and Warren. The railroad agents were men who ensured that their companies didn't take losses due to bandits. Bankers like Wells and Fargo weren't willing to allow their profits to go up in nighttime robberies.

That didn't explain why Sloan was out at her place. He owed his time to the railroad, not some tiny mill in Silver Peak. The room she stood in was just one bunkhouse in a series that he'd used throughout his postings. Sometimes agents stayed a year in one spot before moving on. Some moved every month in an effort to disguise the strength of their numbers from the locals in each town. But Warren and Sloan didn't have the look of the normal agents she'd seen in Silver Peak. There was something far more precise about them. Standing up to some of the miners in town hadn't prepared her for the hard presence that was sitting on the opposite side of the door right now.

And running her father's mill alone this season sure hadn't taught her a thing about dealing with Sloan. With a little huff, she turned and looked at the stove. She was starving. Her belly complained loudly as she looked at the cupboard. Taking his food seemed an insult to her pride, but pride didn't do much for an empty stomach. With another snort of disgruntlement, she moved towards the stove and opened the door on the front of it to take a look at the coals.

She shook her head while she poked the coal in the stove. No, she had a much bigger dilemma to chew on while she waited for Sloan to show back up. Sloan wasn't something she had any clue as to how to deal with and the man would be back. No doubt about it.

She could just wish she wasn't looking forward to it quite so much. Her nipples tingled with little nips of sensation that felt far too good for her to muster any real shame over. The man did make her feel. In all those places that she knew she had but had never spoken about to another living soul. Buried beneath her knickers, that spot he'd touched was begging for another forbidden moment of bliss. The concept of right versus wrong might be firmly instilled in her head, but her body wasn't the least bit interested in her childhood teachings. She wanted to be bare against Sloan's hard male body again and that was the truth.

At least she blushed at the idea of it.

CR

"Three men. Heavy." Jedidiah considered the tracks in the soft dirt a while longer before standing back up. The half-breed didn't raise his voice, he never did. But no one read tracks like the Kiowa did.

Sloan studied the front door of Brianna's house, searching out the little details that would tell him what had happened here last night. Most thieves were sloppy. Their greed made them blind to the evidence they left in their wake. Sometimes, he ran across hardened criminals, but not today. The door was smashed in with the aid of an ax, telling him that whoever had come stealing last night, they'd planned it. A drunken group loose from one of the saloons wouldn't have thought to bring along an ax and Brianna's was sitting neatly above the chopping block in back of her mill.

Hooking his hands into his belt, he surveyed the mess in the front room. Brianna's cupboard was ransacked. A glistening mess of broken jars lay on the floor with the contents oozing among the fragments of glass. There were still a few rows of jars left exactly where Brianna had placed them. Their neat labels all faced forward. But empty shelves proclaimed her loss, a thin layer of dust marking where rows of winter stock had been neatly stored until last night.

"Anything interesting?"

Jedidiah Hancock's voice came from behind him and Sloan stepped aside to let his fellow agent get a look at the pantry. Silence hung over the room for a moment before Jed turned his attention back to him.

"Thief has a sweet tooth."

Sloan nodded agreement. "Nothing but tomatoes and carrots left." The scent of sweet summer berries drifted up from the pile of smashed ones, but there wasn't a single fruit preserve left on any shelf.

Turning around, Sloan noted the disorder of the rest of the home. Every garment Brianna owned was lying on the floor, the drawers still open to reveal their polished insides. The bedding had been torn from the mattress and left in a heap. Mud was tracked through the colorful quilts, marring their bright surface. If there had been even one copper penny in the place, it was long gone. Leaving Brianna the task of rebuilding her life out of the mess left behind. It wasn't an uncommon event in the West. It was even less unfamiliar to women who lived alone in a community that embraced the idea that possession was nine-tenths of the law.

She was lucky to have anything remaining at all. It was strange in a way, because the thief had plenty of time to load up her own wagon with the contents of the cabin. The buckboard was stored in the barn with the single horse her father had left her. Even one horse could have pulled the wagon a few miles, plenty far enough to get a second horse to complete the team. A few days' drive and it would have been simple to sell every last household item to new prospectors. If they only wanted the food, chances were, the culprit was local.

"I doubt they'll be back, at least until next season." Jed's voice was somber with the certain knowledge that Brianna's trouble with the lawless wasn't likely to be a one-time event. As long as she lived alone, she was an easy mark for thieves.

Sloan felt his gut twist. Something far more menacing than anger surged through him. People lost their lives over food more often in the remote towns, but this time, the crime hit him personally. Brianna's face was etched in his memory, just as he'd found her last night, her lips blue from the river and ice clinging to her from head to toe. Even if it was merely a crime of winter supplies, it had almost cost her life. The intentions didn't make a damn bit of difference to him. He itched to hold a rifle on the scum. Men like that needed to face the barrel of a gun. It was the only thing they respected.

The harsh emotion didn't shock him this time. He enjoyed it as it moved through his blood like fine whiskey.

Jed watched him from across the room. "What's the woman to you?" It was a blunt question from a man who had backed him up for too many years. The Indian's dark eyes issued a faint challenge as he waited for him to claim or deny his interest in Brianna.

"She is strong." That was high praise from Jed. It needled him though, because he didn't like any man being attracted to Brianna, even Jed. Especially Jed, half-blooded Kiowa. If the man took an interest in Brianna, he'd hunt her.

"I'll let you know when I decide what she is to me. Until then, she's mine." Sloan turned and left the home. He wasn't going to dwell on his comment. Most of the time, his first instinct was the right one. Maybe it didn't make a whole lot of sense, but that didn't change the warm feeling he got as the warning rolled past his lips. The taste of her kiss lingered in his thoughts. A whole host of other memories rose up from the dark hours of the night and he savored the heat that stiffened his cock in response.

Jed chuckled, moving along behind him. "Women distract men. That is why they are never allowed on a hunt. Warriors know better than to challenge nature."

"Brianna is distracting, I'll give you that. But I'm beginning to enjoy it."

And she was his, at least until he figured out just what his fascination was with her. Jed and Warren would understand.

Jed's hand shot out to catch his arm. The half-breed leveled a harsh look at him. "She will haunt your soul if you taste her. A woman like her will touch your heart with her innocence. There is life in her."

A ripple of anticipation went down his spine in response. His cock twitched as it stirred back to attention. Haunt? No question about it, but the warning felt late. Her kiss was a slow intoxicating venom moving through his blood. "You have that right, my friend."

Jed whistled softly. "You do not understand but I think you are too lucky. Now that she has seen you, there is no chance for me." He returned his eyes to the tracks left from last night. He moved along, reading the faint trail as Sloan battled the need to growl at him for even thinking about his woman.

"Find your own woman."

Jed turned his face toward him. A whisper of amusement touched the half-breed's lips. "You have not claimed her yet. She has not promised you her heart."

"Fat lot you know."

Jed smiled in response. Sloan felt like cussing. A base reaction, one that he wasn't sure how to handle, but he'd figure it out and the only person he needed to help him was Brianna. His lips twitched with amusement as he contemplated her response to that notion. Her spunk was sure to raise its head and in all honesty, he looked forward to the confrontation.

CR

Joseph Corners watched his pa slurp down a jar of jelly like a bowl of chowder. He ate it with a spoon, smacking his lips as he licked them. He didn't stop until he scraped the bottom of the glass.

"Not bad, son." The spoon clattered as it dropped into the empty jar sitting in front of his sire. "Could be better though, if there was a woman here to get to the cleaning. I'd sure enjoy a clean bed."

"She went into the river." Joseph's younger brother Sam snickered as he spilled the information. "That little bitch jumped into the icy water to escape Joe's bed. Better luck next time, brother."

"Shut your mouth, Sam!" Joseph surged forward towards his sibling, but his father's fist connected with his youngest son's nose before Joseph got close.

"Quit your squalling, Sammy. Joseph's just got to chase her down. That's part of the fun. I tumbled your mother a few times before she agreed to marrying me. Nothing better than spirit in a bitch when you mount her. Joseph will bring her around. He's my boy after all."

His pa grinned, showing off his yellow teeth smeared with strawberry jam. He pointed a sticky finger and Joseph leaned closer to listen up to his father. His own nose was still sore from the last time he'd failed to give his father the respect the man demanded from everyone around him.

"Now you just got to be a little more sneaky about it. You made too much noise and had light with ya. Next time, you wait until the full moon and don't let that gal do anything that might kill her. We don't get the mill unless you are married legal-like."

Greed brightened his pa's eyes. The sight of it sent a chill down Joseph's spine, because disappointing his pa was never a good thing. His cock itched for a taste of Brianna Spencer but he had never been real keen on jobs that took too much trouble. Sammy, Will and he had filled up their kitchen with all her preserves and provisions. He wasn't so sure her pussy was worth another night of work. But the look on his pa's face said that the older man wasn't in the mood to hear about what Joseph wanted. His pa wanted that mill. He'd better get Brianna to the church altar or his father's temper was going to thrash his hide something fierce. At least he'd get to fuck her. He wouldn't have to share her pussy with anyone and that would be a first in his life. He'd never owned a woman before. The idea danced in front of him, mesmerizing him.

"Like you said, Pa. I'll be careful."

Joseph turned and rolled into his bunk. He didn't bother to kick off his boots. The inch of mud caked on the worn leather crumbled into his bedding as he stretched out and began to think about having Brianna at his beck and call. Reaching down, he rubbed his swollen cock as he drifted off to sleep and began snoring.

Chapter Five

When he pushed his door open, his bunkhouse smelled like heaven. Sloan hesitated behind the protection of the hard wood as he waited to see just how angry his guest was. Shouldering his way into the room, he scanned the interior with a quick look in case Brianna was waiting to chuck his coffeepot at his head.

She stood on the far side of the room with an expression that should have conveyed her annoyance, but all he noticed was that spunk of hers. Her lips were pressed into a pout and her eyes glimmered with the promise of retaliation. Heat bubbled up from where he'd strapped it down. There was no question of controlling his reaction. It emerged instantly in response to being close to her once more. Last night was too fresh in his brain and his bunk too private to ignore the rise of renewed need.

"You have too much nerve." She'd known that and didn't really need to state it out loud, but her nerves were twitching. Shifting her feet, Brianna bit into her lower lip as she studied Sloan. All her thinking and planning didn't hold up when she faced off with him. Distractions popped up from all over her flesh as her mind insisted on reminding her of just what he'd done with her body last night.

More importantly, how much she'd like to repeat the experience in spite of being at odds with his methods of dealing with her break-in.

He pushed the door shut with a firm hand before his dark eyes returned to survey her. As her gaze traced the wide shoulders that had allowed him to pull her out of a death trap last night, a hint of shame wiggled past her annoyance with being left under Warren's care. "Thank you." She clasped her hands together as her mother had taught her was polite and tried to bleach the annoyance out of her voice before clarifying. "For fishing me out of the river. I certainly appreciate it."

"And warming you up before you ended up dead?"

Her face turned scarlet. "Yes." Her voice failed her miserably as she squeaked like a child caught with her hand in the sugar jar. It was something you craved, in spite of knowing it would rot your teeth. Still, the vision of sticking your finger into those sweet crystals was mesmerizing. Taunting you until you braved the consequences.

There was a hint of something untamed in his eyes as she answered right up concerning those forbidden moments in his bed. Brianna looked at him straight, refusing to duck her head out of some practiced idea of modesty. That flicker of heat in his dark gaze drew her attention completely.

"You shouldn't be thanking me." Sloan's voice was full of reprimand. Brianna frowned at the chastisement. He sounded like he was attempting to shift into the role of parent, but the memory of his kiss made that an inappropriate vision if ever there was one.

"I value my life, which was why I thanked you." Adding a nod to her words, she watched his frown darken. "Being alive this morning sort of has me in the mood to leave the details behind me. What matters is I'm among the living."

His lips twitched as he shrugged out of his duster. With one large hand, he hung it on a hook that was driven into the thick timber framing the doorway. The black oilcloth draped the wall like a slice of midnight that he'd carved out of the heart of the night.

"Good. At least I won't have to listen to you complain about Warren."

Brianna frowned. "That's something altogether different. Placing me under guard is quite out of line."

"Not to my way of thinking." His voice told her that he wasn't willing to budge on the matter. He considered her face for a moment before taking a long step towards her. A shiver shot down her spine as she fought to keep her feet firmly in place. An annoying reaction, but chastising herself didn't change the sensation coursing through her.

His mouth curved up in response. She couldn't seem to control her reactions to him and something flickered in his eyes that said he enjoyed that fact.

"I suppose we'll simply have to agree to being on opposite sides of that issue."

Sloan crossed his arms over his chest as frown lines appeared on his forehead. "As in we agree to disagree?"

Brianna nodded and his eyebrow rose.

"That's just like a woman."

The way he uttered his words made her temper flare back to life. Propping her hands on her hips, she lifted one shoulder. "Well yes, I suppose it is. Men, on the other hand, much prefer to fight, so they never give up a reason to let their fists talk for them. You'd much rather fight than be civilized and understand that sometimes people disagree. I really don't see that as something to boast about."

A deep rumble of amusement shook his chest. His gaze flashed with warning as he closed the distance between them. Brianna lifted her chin as he loomed over her. Sloan's eyes were full of heat as he tapped the end of her nose with the tip of one finger.

"You've got a temper hidden inside your respectable shell. You should be careful who you show that to."

"I call it confidence. Besides, I'm not frightened of you, Sloan." Even if it would have been smarter for her to transform into a mouse whenever he showed up. His mouth was set in a firm line reminding her just how good his kiss made her feel. She'd never believed a man's lips could make her head spin with delight, but Sloan's had. She'd kissed him back too. If she'd cowered or cried, she'd bet he'd cast her one long disgusted look before hightailing it away from her weak-kneed body. A man like Sloan wouldn't waste his time on a woman who couldn't stand up to him.

"You really should be, honey. I'm not a gentleman." His gaze dropped to her lips and the tender skin tingled in response. She caught a whiff of his warm scent. It triggered a response that made her shudder. Heat filled her cheeks instantly, like some signal her body wanted to display in the hopes of attracting his attention. His eyes shifted to her face, lingering on the scarlet stain. He stroked a single finger across the blush. "But I already told you that."

His touch slid all the way across her cheek. It was a deceptive caress, so soft and tempting. The illusion ended as his fingers threaded into her hair and tightened into that grip she recalled so well. Strong and unbreakable, but still painless unless she moved. His head angled as he leaned forward to connect their mouths in another firm kiss. But it wasn't hard. He teased her lower lip with the tip of his tongue before pressing her to open her jaw for a deeper taste.

It felt too good to resist. Brianna let him push her mouth wide as she lifted her hands and allowed her fingertips to explore the hard chest that fascinated her. A low groan shook his torso as an arm clamped around her waist. Her hands slid up to his shoulders as he pulled her against his body, securing her in his embrace. The cotton of his shirt frustrated her. She longed for the warm male skin hidden beneath the garment. His tongue thrust deep into her mouth, teasing her own with a hard stroke.

Brianna shivered as hot need flowed down her body to that spot between her thighs. It throbbed for attention as she twisted towards Sloan, gripping his shoulders in an attempt to get closer. Her skin became alive with acute sensation, causing her to hate her dress and corset. She wanted to be bare for his hands, so that she could enjoy being stroked.

The grip in her hair pulled her away from his kiss. A muffled word got caught behind his clenched teeth as he broke their kiss but didn't relax the arm that bound her to his body. Hunger brightened his eyes as he looked at her like a starving man. She felt his huge body shudder before he let her go.

Brianna bit into her lower lip to contain the little whimper that wanted to spill from her mouth. Being turned loose was like setting out into the snow with your face ruby-red and warm from standing over the coals. The icy wind slapped you like tiny, frozen daggers when you set off without a scarf to protect your face from the harsh elements.

"I need to go home."

Sloan grunted. His gaze moved down her frame before he slowly nodded. "Yes, you do. Before I do something irreversible."

Wicked temptation taunted her to challenge his control. The look on his face said he didn't want to stop touching her and a large part of her wondered just what it would take to push him past his limit. But that was a coward's way. She looked at the floor as she tried to scrape up some composure. Dignity was out of the question, because she flatly didn't want to be honorable or any kind of proper. All she wanted was to press herself back into his embrace and discover just how much better the sensation might get.

Life was somehow more precious today and she wasn't so willing to miss out on anything because of someone else's rules. Her body wanted Sloan to take her down that dark path that was hidden behind shadows of ignorance that all the good wives in town called modesty.

Respectability felt like a poor trade for the delight she knew Sloan could produce with a single touch. But she wasn't willing to taunt him for it and she wasn't quite bold enough to demand it from him. Yet.

"Is my house still standing?"

CR

At least there was something to funnel her frustration into. The harsh reality of looking at bare cupboards stole every scrap of composure she'd dredged up. Her face turned red, this time with her temper. Wrath might be a deadly sin, but at that moment she was a little more interested in handing out a well-deserved thrashing to the thieves who'd stolen her hard work. Most of the fruit had come by way of trade. It was the same as lifting coin out of her purse. A hard hand curled around her upper arm as she rose onto her toes to peer at the few remaining jars in her pantry.

"That glass will cut your feet."

Sloan gave her a tug and she stumbled right back into the middle of the cabin. A hiss escaped her lips as she faced another dilemma brought on by last night's robbery. Food and now shoes, both were necessities. But providing them would prove hard with the river full of ice today. The best she might hope for was hiding the worry seeping into her brain from Sloan. Poor comfort but better than nothing.

"I'll pull down some of my old shoes." Her gaze landed on the rifle resting in the gun rack over her father's bed. She'd pull the weapon down first. She couldn't count on luck to save her life again, so that left cold steel. Sloan didn't miss where her attention went.

"You know how to use that?"

Brianna nodded. She forced her head to move in a firm gesture because she couldn't afford to be timid. Paying the bank note on the mill was apparently not the only hurdle she had to clear in order to maintain her home.

"I'll manage."

A harsh snarl startled her. Jerking her eyes off the rifle, she looked at Sloan. Heavy disapproval darkened his face. "You need to pack up and move into town for the winter. Today. I'll bring a buckboard around to help you."

"No, thank you." Her spine straightened with the aid of her temper. "I'll manage just fine."

"Like you did last night?" Sloan scowled, but it only reinforced her determination. She was not going to collapse into his care.

"That's right, Sloan McAlister." Her hands propped on her hips as she stood firm. "Last night I managed to make sure I didn't end up violated and murdered. Rather decent accomplishments if I do praise my own efforts."

Sloan snaked a hand back out and captured her wrist. He held it secure in his grasp for a long moment, showing her that she didn't have the strength to escape. He yanked her forward and she tumbled into his hard body as he clamped his arm around her waist to hold her captive against him. He cupped her chin and raised her head up until their eyes met. She felt his breath hit her lips as he leaned down towards her.

"Sure about that, Brianna? There's not a whole lot more to bed sport than you ended up getting last night from me. You were on your back with my hand between your thighs."

She slapped him. Her palm cracked across his face as her eyes flared with outrage. He didn't turn his head to ease the force of her blow but kept his eyes locked on her face.

"Stop trying to scare me, Sloan. You're a better man than that. Maybe not a gentlemen, but you don't lack integrity. Don't shame your mother."

An angry handprint appeared on his skin but he didn't flinch or slacken his grip on her. Brianna stared at him, unwilling to back down. Something inside her refused to believe he was anything less than a decent man. She couldn't bear the disappointment of finding out otherwise.

"I told you not to trust me, honey."

The endearment stoked the fire that had begun in his cabin. She melted against him, her curves some sort of perfect fit against his harder male body. Smoothing her fingers over the red spot where she'd struck him, she enjoyed the sensation that rippled down her arm from the skin-to-skin contact. "Trust isn't something you decide about, Sloan. You can just walk out the door, too, if you've got the notion to turn your back and forget you ever laid eyes on me. I didn't decide to trust you, it just grew somewhere inside me. A lot like the idea that I like the way you make me feel when you touch me. I've failed to talk myself out of it. But not from a lack of effort."

"You've got that part right." He shuddered as she stroked his chin again, drawing a harsh breath as she gave in to the temptation to touch him.

"You should tell me to leave." His mouth landed on top of hers before she took a single breath. Her brain refused to continue to dwell on reasons or rules. The scent of his skin was intoxicating, taunting her with just how good it felt to be bare against his body. She reached for his shoulders as she touched his tongue with her own.

A hard male groan shook his chest and it fed her budding confidence. Lifting up on her toes, she sent her tongue along his in a long stroke making delight race down her spine. The arm clamping her to his body shifted and his hand smoothed down past her waist to her bottom. He cupped one cheek through her petticoat and skirt. A little gasp from her broke their kiss while the front of her sex throbbed with demand. It was thick and hot this time, leaving no room for contemplation. Like a starving woman, she pressed her mouth back against his to renew their kiss.

But his kiss was no longer enough. She needed to feel him, like he had stroked her last night. Her hands slid down his chest and lingered when her fingers found his male nipples. She'd seen them, but never touched them. Rubbing them, she felt his chest shudder as a deep sound of appreciation rose from his mouth.

"Go on, honey, touch me."

His voice was husky. Daring her to follow where her hunger dictated. She was drunk on confidence. Unwilling to continue on as head of the household while clinging to girlish ignorance. If she shouldered the load, she wanted to sample the darker pleasures that went along with being an adult.

"Unbutton my shirt." Her fingers stilled on his nipples as her eyes flickered between his button and his face. Sloan gently squeezed her bottom as he watched her decide what to do with his demand. She was a live coal in his grip, but he was enjoying the heat too much to care about the burns it would leave behind. All his well-thought-out reasons didn't make much of a barrier against the pure enjoyment of having her against his body. His cock was hard with need as he caught the delicate scent of her arousal. It rose from her thighs as she unwittingly pressed her hips towards him.

"All right."

The tip of her tongue slid over on her lower lip before she moved her hands to the center button on his shirt. She pushed it through its hole and found the next one. Anticipation tightened his gut as she opened all the buttons above his waist before stroking his chest through his open shirt. Her touch sent bolts of pure fire across every muscle his body contained. It raced down to his cock where it transformed into blinding need.

But he couldn't rush towards that final moment of penetration because he was a slave to the slow exploration of her fingers as she pushed his shirt open to expose his nipples. Her eyes fastened on them as she teased each tip, sending pleasure rippling through him. It was a torture he'd only dreamed of enduring. Even if it killed him, he was going to die a happy man waiting on her whim.

Her mouth went dry as she stroked his chest. His crisp male body hair felt so good between her fingers. She slid her hand all the way up to his nipples and back down to his waistband as she absorbed the pure delight of how different they were. Male and female were opposites, but somehow their bodies combined into a stunning concoction of delight and sensation. She brushed his waistband as indecision filled her. Raising her head, she found his obsidian eyes watching her.

"I think it's your turn."

A small smile lifted his mouth, taking the hard edge off his expression. The fingers clasping her bottom smoothed over her buttock cheek in a soft circle before the hand in her hair released the brown strands.

"You sure about that?"

He didn't sound like he enjoyed asking the question. The resolution in his voice refilled her confidence with the fact that he found her as irresistible as she did him. Stroking his firm abdomen once more, she continued up, stopping when her fingers reached his nipples and she shivered as she contemplated letting him return the touch. Beneath her corset her nipples tingled before tightening into hard points that poked the sturdy poplin of her undergarment. She had never detested the thing so much.

"As sure as I know how to get."

A warm male chuckle was his response. He brushed the side of her neck, sending ripples of enjoyment down her spine.

"That's honest enough, honey." His voice was laced with approval. A far different sort of praise than she had ever received. Hidden in his husky tone was a promise that heightened the excitement racing through her blood. Her heart thumped beneath her breasts in a frantic rhythm that should have alarmed her, but instead she opened her eyes wide so that she wouldn't miss a single detail.

"I like the idea, a whole lot." Rich with promise, his voice sent a shaft of delight through her.

He moved and she gasped when he grasped her waist. He lifted her right off her feet and placed her on the small kitchen table. His bare chest filled her sight as he shrugged off his open shirt and tossed it over a chair. One large hand curled around her face, lifting her chin until their eyes met.

"I shouldn't like the idea." His hand cupped her chin as a frown covered his lips. "But it's the truth that I do."

Indecision flickered in his gaze. Reaching up, she laid her fingers on his firm jaw. His skin was rougher than hers, but it seemed so perfect because they complemented each other. "I like it, too, in spite of trying to talk myself out of it." It might have been one of the most honest statements she'd ever spoken out loud. A person's thoughts were always purely honest, but you learned from your parents to whitewash your words. It just wasn't working with Sloan. Maybe she needed him to understand her. To test out whether or not he wanted her and not some model of a ladies' finishing school.

His hands landed lightly on top of her chest. Her breath caught in her throat as he teased the swells of flesh pushed up by her corset stays. The worn calico of her dress felt too tight as he stroked her. The need to touch him in return filled her. It felt so natural to lift her hands and lay them on his bare sides. His fingers popped the first button on her top open. He moved through the rest of her buttons far faster than she had done with his shirt. There was no hesitation on his part as he pushed her bodice open and right down her arms. Her corset was hooked down the front with laces at the back for practicality. The undergarment pressed her breasts up into a tempting display now that her bodice lay on the table behind her.

"You still sure?" His fingers traced the front closure of her corset. A shiver raced down her back, but she was even more intoxicated than before.

"I'm not sure I'd find the strength to leave even if you told me to." His hard voice sent a ripple of excitement through her. She should have been frightened, but her body leapt at the idea of knowing he wanted her too much to leave. The first hook on her stays opened and he worked the rest with quick fingers. "The sight of you has haunted me."

As an endearment it was perfect. Brianna moaned as he closed a hand around each of her breasts, cupping the tender flesh and rubbing each nipple with his thumbs. His gaze was on her bare torso as he brushed her nipples once more. He kneeled down to lick one hard tip. A cry escaped her lips as heat seared across her nipple. It poured down her body to that spot at the top of her sex. She wiggled on the tabletop as sensation made it impossible to remain still. A soft chuckle came from her partner as he slid a hard arm around her body, pressing her back over his arm. The position thrust her nude breasts upwards into a display that made her blush.

"Perfect. So sweet and perfect." He growled the words before sucking one nipple. His arm held her tight as she gasped. She was suddenly unbearably hot. The layers of her dress a prison she was desperate to break out of. The hard sucking on her nipple sent more heat into her lower body as she clawed at his biceps. Her nipple, all shiny and wet from his ministrations, popped out of his mouth when he pulled his mouth away from her breast. The cloudy afternoon chill brushed across the wet skin making her gasp at the contrast.

He picked her up and set her feet back on the floor. There was a pull and a tiny tear as he yanked her skirt and petticoat open. He pushed all the fabric down over her hips. It puddled around her ankles and knees as he captured the back of her head and raised her face up to his. His eyes glittered with determination. Hard and frightening in a way, but also promising. She hummed with delight as she stroked his chest and leaned forward to lick one of his nipples.

He cussed and the hand in her hair tightened, sending tiny nips of pain down her neck. But the reaction only fueled her determination to return the pleasure he'd just given her. Angling her head she licked the small flat nipple before closing her lips around it and sucking. His chest shook as his breath rasped between clenched teeth. He released her hair and she moaned as he pushed her knickers over the curves of her hips. Once over her thighs, her last garment slithered down to join the puddle around her knees.

Sloan picked her up, leaving her clothing in a small heap. A moment later he laid her in her bed, scraping the disorderly bedding aside. His boots hit the floor as he jerked them off with quick motions of his hands. She heard his belt buckle unlatch as he pushed his pants off.

She caught a glimpse of his bare backside before he rolled her into the bedding without letting her look at his cock.

But she was still in heaven as his chest covered her breasts. His mouth found hers and his tongue thrust forward to stroke her own. One large hand smoothed a path from her breast to her belly and then lower, to the top of her sex. He pushed right into the delicate folds protecting her clit. Searching for that spot he'd rubbed last night. Her body quivered almost violently when his fingertip touched it. A thin cry broke through their kiss as her head thrashed with the abundance of the sensation. Pleasure tightened under his finger as he rubbed her clit, increasing the speed a little at a time.

"Spread for me, honey."

Her eyes widened at the pure wickedness of his words. It was the honest truth that she had never considered that anyone actually spoke out loud about the things that went on between a man and women in bed. But it excited her, hearing the words in his husky tone. Her thighs obeyed before she felt the blush heating her face. The fingertip in her slit rubbed the little bud at the top of her sex as the folds of flesh covering it moved apart when she spread her legs.

"Wider." He didn't wait for her to comply but rolled slightly to one side of her body, pushing her legs right up so her bent knee was above her waist. A startled sound emerged from her lips but she was unsure just what it was. Alarm, excitement—Brianna couldn't decipher it. All she knew was the finger between her thighs was driving her insane. Her hips lifted off the bed towards his hand as

111

need swept aside everything but the desire to have him unleash that sweet pleasure once again with his touch.

"I'm not going to leave you a virgin this time."

One thick finger touched the entrance to her body along with his words. Her hips twitched towards the touch and the motion sent the tip into her passage. Hard desire filled her sheath as she realized how good it felt to have something inside her. She suddenly understood what she craved from him. It was dark and unspoken, but she was no stranger to what happened when a female was mounted.

The surprise was how much her body enjoyed being penetrated. The need pulsing around that finger filled her with boldness. Extending her leg, she drew her calf and ankle over his leg. His eyes closed to slits as his breath rasped between clenched teeth in a low sound of male enjoyment. Cupping his chin, she sent her leg back for another stroke across his cock. His obsidian eyes flashed open as her fingers closed around his jaw.

"I sure hope you're planning to finish this." Her voice was too husky for any more patience.

"I didn't say we'd finish anything today, honey. But you won't be a virgin any longer."

He raised his head to lock stares with her once more. His hand left her passage and she ached to be filled. Hunger drew his face taut. "It will take a lot more than one ride to finish this. I promise you that."

The thick head of his cock nudged her. His hips spread her thighs wide as he caught a handful of her hair to hold her steady and at his command. "But it's a damn good place to start."

He drove his length into her with a slow thrust. Her hips lifted for the penetration as her body stretched. Pain ran through her as the breath rushed out of her lungs too fast. A hand curled around the side of her hip to hold her in place. He held most of his body weight on one elbow and her chest rose as she gasped. He moved in the same moment, pulling out of her body and thrusting back up into her. He pressed deeper the second time. Pain nipped all along her passage as it was stretched. Two tears spilled down the sides of her face as the pain suddenly diminished. A soft kiss captured one tear and then the other as her body relaxed and sweet delight began to pulse through her.

Reaching for her lover, she lifted her hips towards him. A hard growl hit her ear as he rose up, allowing more of his weight to rest on her. It completed the contact she craved as he began to move slowly between her thighs. Each stroke drew the length of his cock along that little button at the top of her slit.

Pleasure shot up into her belly as she worked her hips up harder and faster to meet his thrusts. Everything twisted and tightened around his cock until it burst in a shower of lightning so hot and intense she listened to her cry as though someone else were screaming. The bed ropes creaked and groaned as her partner bucked between her thighs. He thrust hard and with faster motions until his harsh groan covered up her whimpers. Sloan pressed his length deep and she felt the eruption of his seed filling her. The bed rocked gently as he collapsed onto his elbows, both their chests heaving, lungs striving to keep up with their hearts.

A soft hand brushed her hair out of her face before a kiss was laid against her lips. "No, honey, one ride is not going to finish this." Brianna opened her eyes to see a hard man looking at her. She shivered at the sight, because she faced the man who could hold his own against any odds. But his fingers were so gentle as they smoothed her hair back from the trails her tears had left on her cheeks. "Not by a long shot."

Sloan rolled and pulled her against his side. One hand secured her hips flush with his body as his fingers cupped the side of her bottom. She should have been outraged to have a hand on her fanny but it felt so intimate that a small sigh left her lips as her eyelashes fluttered shut.

She could just worry about everything later. Her ruined winter stores, the destroyed house and her reckless embrace of a man she should have steered clear of. None of it seemed more important than the contentment seeping through her as he held her. The sound of his heart filled her ear, calming her like some sort of music.

Sloan slipped into slumber right along with her. His mind at peace for the first time in a long spell. She nuzzled against his chest and he tightened his grip. It was a moment of perfection that he'd never suspected the world could contain. No, it wasn't finished, but it was a fine place to start.

Chapter Six

The afternoon sun wasn't going to let her linger in slumber. Brianna smoothed a last stroke along her partner's chest before raising her head. She caught the faint scent of preserves on the breeze and resigned herself to getting on with cleaning up the mess in her pantry. Like any dream, you had to wake up to the harsher side of life at some point.

Sloan's large hand rested on her bare shoulder. He moved it slowly down her arm before sitting up and taking her with him. He held onto her wrist and turned her palm up so that he could look at it. A frown marred his face as he glared at the angry red wounds decorating her skin.

"It's nothing." Giving a pull, she tried to take her palm out of his view. He held tight as he shifted his gaze to her face.

"It sure as hell is something. Make sure you douse those with alcohol." His face remained taut. "Do you have any whiskey in the house?"

"No. My father wouldn't spend money on anything that wasn't a necessity until the bank note was paid in full."

A grunt of approval came from Sloan. "I'm growing fond of your sire." He slipped his legs over the side of the bed and stood. He looked back at her with longing in his dark gaze. "I need to take a shift on the rail dock."

Brianna caught the quilt out of habit before it slithered down to leave her breasts exposed. Sloan's eyes filled with amusement. He angled his head and placed a solid kiss against her lips. A hard promise flickered in his eyes when he lifted his mouth away. "I will be back tonight. I'll bring something for your hands."

Listening to his words released the little knot of tension hiding between her shoulders. She hadn't even realized she was worried until he spoke. A naughty little grin lifted her lips as she watched him reach for his boots.

"Does that mean I can offer you dinner without raising your hackles?"

A male snort was her reply. He stepped into his boots and pulled them up to his calves while frowning at her. "You don't take warnings very well, honey."

Brianna rose to her knees. She let the quilt go and it fell to the surface of the bed. His eyes focused on her nipples and he lost his reprimanding expression. She enjoyed the moment, savoring her ability to change his mood just by being herself. "And you don't take teasing very well, Sloan McAlister. Everyone needs a little humor in their day."

The look that passed over his face shocked her. Sloan had always struck her as so strong that the flicker of vulnerability stood out. A hint of need in his eyes made her heart twist, because she had never considered that a man like him might get lonely. Or that she wielded the power to entrance him. It was a sure bet that he'd shared bed sport with far more practiced women.

"Maybe you're right about that. It has been a long time since someone teased me just for the sake of placing a smile on my face." A grin graced his lips for a moment as he worked the buttons on his shirt. He tucked the tail into his trousers and turned around.

"Oh... So, you do know how to smile. Thank you for the revelation."

One of his dark eyebrows rose as his gaze lingered on her nude breasts. She resisted the urge to cover them with her hands, keeping her hands on the quilt instead. He made her feel so pretty, two tears stung her eyes.

"We'll see about revelations when that sun sets tonight. I need to put in some work, woman, so stop tempting me to go lazy and crawl back into bed."

He pulled her father's rifle off its resting pegs and lifted it up to look down the sights of the barrel. He moved it in a steady, practiced motion around the room before lowering it to peer into the trigger housing.

"Needs cleaning. Badly." There was the ring of chastisement in his voice for allowing the weapon to get rusty. Like a mother sounded when she caught her sons with dirty hands at the supper table.

He set it next to the pantry. "Keep it at hand, and I do mean at hand." A hard look hit her square in the face.

"Your father's late arrival is the talk of the town. You need to keep that weapon with you at all times."

"I suppose you're correct." Stepping out of her bed, Brianna winced at the tenderness between her thighs. Sloan's eyes caught the little telltale expression, but she shrugged and stepped around him to where her clothes still lay in a puddle on the floor.

"I mean it, honey. Don't take chances while I'm working."

A little ripple of something went through her, a crazy mixture of excitement and disbelief. Sloan didn't miss the indecision as she tried to decide what she thought about his intention to return. A solid arm clamped around her waist as he stepped towards her. She ended up in his embrace again as he held her chin in the palm of one hand.

"I will be back, honey." The expression on his face was as firm as the first time she'd met him. Determination stared back at her until he pressed a kiss onto her mouth before releasing her.

Sloan stepped out the doorframe into the fresh snow. He looked back at Brianna. She formed her lips into a faint pout before closing the door. He waited for the bar to be pushed into place before forcing his boots forward. It was the first time he'd dragged his feet away from a woman.

The way he enjoyed the feeling surprised him. Something like he'd had an empty spot in his chest that

118

he was noticing because it was full today. Yeah, he'd be back and Brianna would get used to that. It was going to be his pleasure to help her every step of the way.

The snow didn't melt on his shoulders today. Brianna shut the door as she watched his black duster spot with white flakes. Patches of snow lay on the ground. By tomorrow there would be nothing but a sea of mud between her home and town. A really bleak thought when she turned and added the sight of her ransacked home to it. An entire year of work gone in a single night. It was almost too much to grasp.

Maybe insanity was creeping into her brain. A fair number of settlers succumbed to craziness. The harsh land coupled with the long periods of keeping company with only yourself had broken more than one mind.

The dark stain marring her bed sheet made her smile. No, she'd been in command of her wits the entire time, even if she did admit to being overwhelmed. That wasn't insanity—the only sin there was lack of self-control. On her way across the room, she stopped and pulled the soiled sheet off the mattress. She waited for shame to tug on her conscience, but it couldn't get a grip. No, she had enjoyed it too much. Never once in her adult life had she ever believed that any act might be so satisfying. If that made a fallen woman, she would wear the label proudly. The spot between her thighs ached as she got on with cleaning. While the snow fell and drifted higher, working the pump drove away the chill. But her hands complained bitterly as each little wound shot pain up her arms. There wasn't a worse day to tend to the laundry, but she only had one sheet for the larger bed, and fallen woman or not, she still had her pride. Sloan McAlister wasn't going to return to a dirty bed—not in her home the man wasn't. She grinned at her own "house pride". Placing a kettle on the stove, she stirred up the coal to heat water for her laundry so the fabric would release the stain.

A little frown broke through her humor. She really had no reason to count on him. Sloan wasn't the settling-down sort of man. Her heart clenched with pain and it made her gasp. Caring so much was unwise. Her heart was too tender and it wouldn't take much to smash it. But events had conspired against her, thrusting her into contact with him in spite of knowing she was better off steering clear of him.

But she wasn't alone in the muddle. Sloan had a mighty hard time ignoring her, too. That might not ease a heartache when he left Silver Peak, but for the moment it kept her humming instead of crying.

Putting her house to rights kept her busy. She almost ignored the need to check her mill house. Too many things on her mind. Adding a list of repairs on the mill house that needed doing before spring didn't appeal at all. Shaking her head at her own thoughts, Brianna pulled the bar up and went to check on her grinding mill. The sheet rippled in the wind and she fingered the fabric to test for dampness. Her clothesline was strung between two ancient oak trees. Their bark was thick and their branches twisted, but it kept her laundry out of the snow.

The wind might be icy cold, but it did the job of drying decently enough.

She pushed the door to the mill house open slowly. Dust from the ground grain sparkled, even in the meager sunlight. The lamp she'd worked by still sat exactly where she'd left it, all of the oil burned. But the bags of barley flour were missing. Stepping into the mill, she frowned as she reached for the little tin sitting above the lamp. It was heavy in her hand and opening the lid revealed a small stack of silver dollars. Surprise whipped through her as she counted the coin. Jimmy Green had left her payment. That meant the two sacks of flour had been waiting for him when he came by.

That added a new twist to her nighttime visitors. They'd left only the vegetables and now the newly ground flour. All of the items she might have expected thieves to take were still in her home. Things like scissors and cooking knives or her new fabric. The iron cooking pots and the spices above the pot-bellied stove, even the soap that had been spilled on the back bedroom floor were all things she expected to lose because it couldn't be traced to her. Things you could find in any kitchen or miner's camp. But they represented money, almost more than the silver coin in her hand. In a small town like Silver Peak, you needed money and luck to get what you wanted. The local mercantile didn't always have supplies on the shelf. It would take months for cast-iron pots to make it across the wagon trails and no one undertook the trip in winter. Robberies were more prevalent this time of year as push came to shove and men were reduced to stealing in order to survive.

Her heart twisted as her father's face sprang to mind. Her father wouldn't be returning anytime soon. If he was alive out there, he'd hole up for the winter now that the snow had arrived. Loneliness swept through her in a dense wave that might have dragged her down into despair if Sloan's voice didn't echo in her memory. She frowned. Maybe she was drawn to him because of loneliness. A harsh fact, but also a possible truth. In four short days, she'd offered him her body when the idea had never entered her thoughts before.

It was a tangle, to be sure. How did any woman know the difference between affection and lust? She'd mistakenly believed that only men suffered from that affliction, but her own body seemed just as caught in the storm created by passion.

"The river's frozen today." A sickening snicker followed that comment as Brianna jerked her head around. Joseph Corners grinned at her like a hyena. His tongue appeared and swiped over his lower lip. Dread washed down her spine as she instantly heard Sloan's parting words.

Keep the rifle at hand...

"You won't be swimming away this time."

Her father's gun was still leaning against the doorframe in the main cabin. Joseph's amusement cut through her self-directed anger.

"Joseph Corners, you have some nerve!"

Joseph didn't take her chastisement very well. A look of panic invaded his eyes, but a snort of amusement from the man behind him turned his face beet red. His hand sailed out and struck her across the face. Her entire head snapped to the side with the force of the blow. Her vision became a shower of bright sparks as her ears rang. She caught her body against one round wall as she tried to make her eyes work.

"Now you listen up, Brianna. I ain't the sort of husband that'll be taking sass from your mouth. No woman's that pretty. You'll be respecting me sure enough. Else you'll feel the back of my hand until you mind your mouth with me."

Her eyes rounded with horror at the word *husband.* Joseph's intention to wed her was even more repulsive than it had been back on the dock. She shuddered with distaste as her mind considered having this man in bed with her, touching her, pressing his foul-smelling hands against her bare skin. It horrified her especially now that she had her encounters with Sloan to compare it to.

"Over my dead body," she snarled at him, willing the vermin out of her sight. "Get off my father's land."

"This here is going to be my mill." Greed glittered in Joseph's eyes and it truly frightened her. Men could kill over greed. More than one miner had lost his life when he struck gold and someone else wanted it bad enough to commit murder.

Joseph clamped a dirty hand around her arm as he shouldered his way past her blows. His body might have been plump, but it was strong and her fist hurt as she swung at his head while yanking on her arm. None of her struggles did any good. A rough blanket wrapped around her as a scream of pure outrage left her lips. Struggling against the dense fabric, she gasped as a rope began to wind around her trapped arms.

It was just too damn easy for them to capture her. Helplessness flooded her as she kicked and turned, trying to thrash against her bindings, but Joseph and his friends only tightened the ropes. Her lungs didn't have enough space to keep up with her racing heart. Blackness clouded her vision and she stilled out of desperation to remain awake.

"Now that's better." Her feet left the floor as Joseph clicked his tongue in approval. "You'll settle down just fine, once you understand who's wearing the britches between us."

His bride-to-be screamed something but it got muffled in the horse blanket. Joseph felt his cock thicken with anticipation. She sent her foot towards him, but missed and he licked his lip as his lust heated up. Nothing better than a woman that wiggled while you fucked her. Dead weight beneath a man could turn his cock soft. He was a lucky man for noticing how good a bride Brianna Spencer would make. All the other bastards in town were going to envy him when he paraded down the street with her on his arm, obedient and devoted to him.

Sammy held the wagon cover open and he and Will pushed Brianna's squirming body into the center of the bed. He stopped long enough to tie another length of rope around her legs to keep her from kicking the side of the buckboard. They didn't need nobody hearing any racket. With another shove he pushed her body into the center and moved a few crates in front of her. A smile split his face as he heard her muffled voice, but no one would hear anything once the wagon was in motion.

"Get that cover tied down. Dark is coming early with this snow."

Brianna swallowed her fear. Panic was only going to increase her odds of ending up in a bad situation. Her eyes couldn't even make out the blanket anymore now that there was no light, but she smelt it sure enough. The old wool stank of rot and horses. She was grateful for having a strong stomach or the stench would have nauseated her. Well, it was a fine fit for its owner. Joseph turned her stomach, too. Leaving the rifle behind had been sure stupidity and that mistake kept her company as the wagon began to rock along the road. She strained against her bindings, but they held true as Joseph continued to haul her away like a prize he'd found.

The only problem being, she really was caught in his trap.

ℭℜ

No light shone from Brianna's house. Sloan pulled his horse up as he stared at the dark cabin. Even with the window boarded up, light should peek out from beneath the door. If Brianna had rolled a blanket up and pushed it against the door to keep the snow chill off the floor, there would be light winking at him from the top of the doorframe. His gut twisted as he forced himself to remain in the dark shadows while he scanned the area. It was silent, most of the wildlife deep in their burrows to wait out the snow. New snow reflected the moonlight, casting everything in a silver light.

Pulling his rifle out of his saddle, he swung one leg over his horse's head and slid down to his feet. Gathering the reins in one hand, he kept his rifle steady. He kept close to his horse, using the animal as a shield as he eased forward. Not a bad gamble, since horses were worth more than most men's lives out west. Thieves would think mighty hard before taking a shot that might hit a healthy mount they could sell once they killed the owner.

A light-colored piece of fabric flapped in the wind. The sound of cloth whipping was the only thing he heard as he drew close enough to make out what it was. His gut twisted further as he recognized the bed sheet. His brain instantly fired up at the sight of it. Only one reason Brianna would have washed it with half the daylight gone. He reached for the front door, striding forward to lean his shoulder into it. The cabin was dark and still, the coals in the stove covered in a good inch of ash. His frown deepened as he considered the rifle leaning against the doorframe exactly where he'd left it.

He was going to blister her bottom when he got her back home.

Sloan didn't bother to question the idea of spanking Brianna. It was an impulse, one that rose from his deepest soul. You didn't argue with that kind of response. Maybe he didn't understand what he felt for her and it sure didn't make much sense to be so attached to a woman he'd met four days ago. But women didn't make sense, one reason he stayed away from their church socials and picnics. A man made it through life real good up until he encountered a female who stirred his interest. That was when he started acting dumb. Shaking his head Sloan walked past the sheet and cussed. His temper boiled until all that remained was thick rage. Brianna was his woman and the son of a bitch who'd taken her would find out just how big a mistake it was to mess with anything Sloan considered his.

Chapter Seven

"You done all right, my boy. All right indeed."

The horse blanket finally left her face and Brianna snarled. She didn't much care if it was by far one of the most unladylike sounds she had ever made. Her temper was in full steam and she wouldn't be surprised if Joseph saw the white vapor rising from her ears.

"Yup, Pa. I done thought about what you said about the light and the way I figured it, maybe sneaking up there in the daytime was the perfect solution. What with the storm and all, nobody was around to even notice. That snow is going to drift deep tonight, so no one will bother looking in on her until it melts next spring."

"Well now, son, you're a bright one all right." Joseph's father smirked at her. His teeth were yellow, like his son's, and it was abundantly clear why Joseph had fallen into being a slob. His father's stench wrinkled her nose. That unwashed scent that built up after months of a man not even washing his hands before supper.

But the cabin she stood in looked just perfect for its inhabitants. The table was piled high with probably every dish the family owned. Stale food decorated the dirty bowls and plates while crumbs sat in piles on the portion of the tabletop that wasn't being taken up by dishes. Her eyes narrowed as she spotted several of her own jars discarded among the mess, spoons still sticking up out of them. The pure gluttony of the way the preserves had been eaten enraged her. They'd gorged on the preserves like animals falling on food with no thought to spreading out the wealth. They'd just converged and ate like a pack of scavengers.

"You thieving mongrels!"

While she was still looking at her demolished winter stocks Joseph's father's hand collided with her jaw. The man kept his fist closed and pain shot into her head and traveled down her backbone as her head whipped around.

"Now, Pa, I told you I like her pretty face," Joseph whined at his sire, but didn't take any action that might place him in the line of his pa's fists.

His pa turned and grunted. "Better teach her to mind that mouth, my boy. I ain't never taken no sass from a woman yet. Ain't planning on starting."

Her hand shook as she rubbed her jaw. Feeling returned with an ache that promised her a bruise later. Joseph's father's eyes glowed with his enjoyment of seeing her hurt under his treatment. "It ain't thieving, girl. You are going to marry up with my boy, so it's just a case of you providing for your family." He flashed his yellow teeth at her once again and raised his fist towards her in a clear threat. "But you better get one thing straight. I don't much care if you're black and blue, just so long as you respect me. This here is my house and that mill is going to be a mighty fine addition to the family. You'll honor me as a father or feel my hand."

"I am not going to marry your son." Her voice was low, but not because of any fear. Her jaw was stiff and pain radiated from every little move she made.

"Well now, I'll just leave that little matter between the two of you." Another flash of yellow teeth and Joseph's father lowered his eyes to look at her breasts. He swiped his tongue over his lower lip and looked like a starving mongrel. "Too bad I've got to give you to the boy. Been a long time since I got a taste of honey, but I don't figure the parson would believe you got a soft heart for an old man like me. Got to have the churchman believing so we gets that mill. I can buy me a whole lot of pussy with money from that mill. That leaves your ass for my boy here. He's going to have you and I just might sit right here and watch him plant a baby in you. Bet a wedding will sound a whole lot better once that's done happened. You can't hold back nature."

Her skin crawled. As long as she lived, Brianna was going to be grateful for the impulse that had seen her laying down with Sloan. What did losing her virginity to a man who wasn't her husband matter when she might well be facing the rough handling of Joseph Corners? Her body shuddered as she clutched her secret close and held onto it to keep her desperation at bay. She would find a way out of the filthy cabin. Somehow, she'd manage to escape or kill one of them in the trying.

"Have fun, boy. I'll see to the team while you welcome your bride home."

Joseph's father smacked his lips before he left the cabin. The two younger sons followed, leaving her to face Joseph. The man didn't frighten her. No, the sight of his stained shirt only fueled her temper as her jaw ached.

"Kiss me." Joseph tried to sound demanding, but he reminded her of a brat screaming for a sugar candy.

"You are insane, Joseph, if you think I'd be kissing anyone who's hit me." It was a brave stand to take. Half the wives in town wouldn't dare lay down any opinion like that before their husbands. Striking a wife wasn't any cause for concern as long as you didn't do real damage.

"I think you'll be kissing me and a whole lot more." Joseph's eyes lit with lust as he ran a hand down to his crotch, a disgusting gesture. There was a pop as he opened his trousers and pulled his erection into view. His protruding belly made it harder to see, but she shivered as nausea filled her. His exterior had been repulsive, his cock was flatly disgusting. The idea of letting it anywhere near her body caused her knees to press tightly against one another. She suddenly understood just why medieval brides had committed suicide rather than consummate their marriages. If the groom looked like Joseph, she'd demand to be sent to a convent, too! Better hours on her knees at prayer than spreading her thighs for his use.

Joseph snickered and worked his hand up and down his erection. "You's going to do everything I tell you. When

I tell you to get on your knees and suck my cock...you'll do it real quick like."

"Joseph, I am not your wife." She tried to keep her voice low. Maybe Joseph would mistake that for respect. His father passed by the dingy front window of the cabin, reins wrapped around his fist. He didn't glance towards the cabin. Her only hope was to lull Joseph into a false sense of victory. But she refused to touch his cock. She wasn't that desperate and she was willing to beg God to let her die before being that broken.

"But you will be." He moved faster than she thought he could. Gripping the back of her hair and pulling. Pain shot down her spine as she braced her bound hands against his chest to hold him away. Mere inches separated them. It would be so easy for him to rape her. Recognition of just how helpless she was against his strength made her angry, but it didn't change the harsh reality. Men were stronger than women. His foul breath hit her nose and she gasped at the stench.

"Now you listen to Joseph." His hand pulled her hair harder until her face was angled towards his. His eyes were full of lust as he ground his erect cock against her belly. She stumbled back until the wall stopped her. Joseph pressed his body against her and leered down into her face.

"You're going to lift your pretty clean skirt anytime I tell you to. You'll obey me like a well-trained bitch because every morsel of food you get will come from my hand. You won't even get a blanket if I don't like the way you look at me. In a few months your belly is going to swell up and you'll be mighty happy to get married." He pressed his cock against her and planted a sloppy kiss against her mouth. Brianna clamped her jaw tight against the vile invasion and Joseph snickered at her resistance.

"You ain't the first bitch I ever broke, just the first human one." He stuffed his cock back into his trousers and closed up his fly. "But I don't see it making much difference. Once your belly's good and empty and your skin cold as ice... Well, you'll be a whole lot more friendly. Mark my words. By tomorrow sunrise, I bet you're going to feel like being much nicer to me. My cock will look just fine when you're starving for a slice of bread."

He grasped her wrist and dragged her towards the far side of the cabin. A pair of thick iron shackles hung from a bolt driven through one of the trees that formed the outer wall of the cabin. Joseph yanked her arm forward and clamped the chilled iron around one wrist. The chain made a horrible noise as he grabbed the second manacle. Brianna flailed at him but he shouldered her into the corner and snapped the second iron shackle in place.

"Now that's better. Got these here shackles from a Chinese fellow that uses them on the girls he brings over for the cribs." Joseph sniffed before grinning at the sight of her locked in his slave chains. He reached forward and ripped her top open. The buttons went scattering onto the floor as she tried to twist away from his hands. He grabbed her skirt as she turned, ripping at the calico until he flung the ruined garment across the room. Her petticoat didn't last very long with his hands clawing at it, but when he pulled the shredded cotton away, she lifted a leg and kicked out at his groin.

"You bitch!" His hand rose to deliver another blow, but he stopped before landing it. His chest shook with laughter instead as he rubbed his bruised cock. "Guess you aren't too hungry yet." His eyes moved over her exposed legs, clad in nothing but a pair of flannel knickers and knee socks. She felt dirty just from the path his eyes took over her limbs and back up to where her corset was showing through her ruined bodice. "That'll change soon enough. You'll be mighty happy to share my bed after a few nights shivering in your bloomers."

"Joseph, this is insane. You're a human being."

"So what?" He reached for one of her wrists and pulled it against the iron bracelet holding her prisoner. A soft cry escaped her lips when he tried to pull her hands through the shackle, but the bones of her hands were too large to fit. The edge bit into her flesh. Joseph grunted approval before he moved away. He kicked her ruined dress and petticoat across the room, well out of her reach.

"You look just like one of them Chinese crib whores. Better be glad you got's something worth marrying for or I just might keep your ass right here and sell it to every trapper that comes by. White whores go for more than Chinese. Maybe I'll sell you anyway, after I know you're growing my baby. Don't see why you can't earn me a little more silver, since I'm feeding you. But I want to know whose baby you birth under my roof."

Brianna pressed against the rough wall in self-defense. The horrible truth was almost too much to grasp. Joseph snickered before he dropped a blanket on top of her ruined dress. "Now there's a nice sight for you to look at while your fingers go numb from the night cold. I'm going to leave it all right here." He snickered again before turning his back on her. The chill from the open door brushed her legs, making her shiver. The bolt that held her shackles was driven into the wall at her waist level, allowing enough chain for her to sit on the dirty floor. Lowering her body, she hugged her knees close to her chest to stay warm. The chains rattled against themselves as she stared at the rusty manacles. The implements of slavery were harsh reminders that many men didn't quibble over taking away the rights of others. She'd only heard of cribs, but the stories were bad enough. Chinese men worked harder for the same pay as white men or even colored men. The Chinese took the most dangerous jobs, often ending up dead as they set the blast charges on the railroad construction tunnels.

Chinese women were worse off than their male counterparts. Unfortunate Chinese girls were sold by their families in China and shipped across the ocean where they were locked into wooden cages called cribs. Any man with coin could pay her keeper and rape her at will. It wasn't a legal practice, but in the territories the practice flourished. Their keepers would slit their throats rather than have the law catch them. Without a witness, there was no trial. Lawmen often arrived too late to save the lives of the unlucky girls.

Her chains rattled as a faint tremor traveled over her body. Right now, she wasn't much better off. It was a somber moment as she considered the harsh realities of her dilemma. Was her will stronger than her flesh? It was easy to say yes, but backing up that claim would be a test of her endurance. She feared dying in the attempt more. Life was a beautiful thing. That thought was especially clear now that she faced the idea of freezing to death instead of catering to Joseph's demands. A shudder of revulsion went through her as she considered his cock. She did prefer the cold to touching that flesh.

Hearing that demand in Sloan's voice would have made her shiver with excitement...

She didn't waste any energy debating the wisdom of thinking about Sloan. A surge of warmth went through her as she let his image fill her mind. One thing Joseph had taught her was the power of her own confidence. Indirectly the slob had shown her that one freely bestowed kiss was worth ten stolen ones. She wasn't a maiden any longer because she'd made a gift of her innocence to the man of her choosing. Clamping her into slave irons showed her the value of indulging in her passion for Sloan. The railroad agent might disappear into the night, smashing her heart as he went, but she would never reproach herself for surrendering her innocence to him. Her body was hers to share, the only person she needed to even that out with was God.

And she sure did like the idea of knowing that Joseph Corners couldn't take her virginity. A smile curved her lips as she considered it justice well suited to the man and his thieving family.

Besides luck was a double-sided coin. It flipped on you without warning. It was just possible she would never see Sloan again. The chains around her wrists were hard and real. No one would have any clue as to her fate. If she died right against this wall, Joseph would bury her body and cover up any trace of his crime.

At least, he would never be able to take away the favor she'd given Sloan. Chastity was a woman's gift to bestow. Men had tried to force it from them for centuries. Joseph couldn't steal her free will.

A sense of calm washed over the panic that had tried to strangle her. She would survive this. Somehow, someway. She would not give up. Not even as she drew her last breath.

CSR

"Smell good?"

Brianna didn't answer Joseph. The pop and sizzle from the iron pot on the stove didn't bother her too much. It was the red glow of the coal that captivated her. She was too far away to feel the warmth radiating from those red-hot coals. The cabin was made only of trees that had been stripped of their bark and used to construct the walls. There was a second-floor loft above her, made of smaller trees. Mud had been packed into the groves between each tree trunk to help keep the weather out, but chunks of it lay in piles along the wall. No one among Joseph's kin seemed to take maintenance any more seriously than cleaning.

The winter air seeped in, chilling her as she tried to hug her legs tighter. The front door of the cabin let in huge gusts of snow-chilled air every time it opened. Her knickers and socks were poor coverage against the dropping temperature. But maybe, she could scrap a little ice through the gap between the logs, just a bit to hold back her thirst. Picking at the mud, she tried to loosen another chunk of it.

"Nothing like bacon on a cold night." Joseph smacked his lips as he chomped down on a thick slice of cured ham shank. He shook his head like a huge dog did after being fed. "Got a piece for you, wife, if you want to be nice."

Brianna turned her face towards the wall. Her belly grumbled but she preferred hunger.

Joseph *tsked* under his breath. "You sound awful hungry. That belly is good and empty, isn't it?" She heard his boots hitting the floor as he came closer. The scent of ham grew stronger and more tantalizing with each footfall. "Bet you're thirsty, too."

A hand gripped her hair, tugging her head around to face a piece of ham. He dangled the roasted meat in front of her nose as the scent filled her senses and her belly rumbled loudly.

"Say 'fuck me, Joseph' and it's yours."

She snarled at him instead. The hand holding her hair tightened, making her cry out with the pain. He stooped down until his mouth was right in front of hers. He stuffed the ham into his mouth and chewed it with huge motions of his jaw as he forced her to keep her face level with his. Shutting her eyes didn't keep her from hearing his lips smack or smell the scent of that meat. Opening her eyes, she shoved her foot into his unprotected crotch again.

"Shit!"

Joseph rolled away from her. His cussing made her smile as she recognized her own power. She might be the one wearing chains, but he couldn't force her to like him.

A second later, a hard smack landed on her face. This time she laughed at his abuse, smiling as she tasted blood on her tongue. Joseph frowned at her glee.

"We'll just see how you feel after a night in your knickers. You don't get nothing until you ask me to fuck your pretty little pussy. Not even water."

Her humor died away as she hugged her legs tight. She shivered as she pictured the snow right on the other side of the tree-trunk wall. Only a foot of wood separated her from ice. The idea was hypnotic in a fashion, drawing her towards a dream world where everything sparkled on millions of icy crystals all full of color and wonder... She let it carry her away, because it was so much more inviting than looking at the ugly reality of Joseph.

CR

"Can't help you."

Sloan held his tongue as the bartender picked up a glass and began to polish it. His temper was paper thin, but there was a finesse to prying information out of a barkeep. The man glared at Jed before spitting on the floor.

"No breeds in my place."

Jed's face didn't betray a single emotion, but Sloan fought to keep his own temper leashed in the face of the bigotry. The West was full of it. Indian, Chinese and the black man were all harnessed for labor but resented by the same men who wanted them breaking their backs in the sun. Jed simply turned and pushed out the shutters that served as doors. Sloan returned his attention to the barkeep.

"Sure you can't help us find that homestead?" Sloan placed a small leather pouch on the bar and fingered it so that the coins inside clinked against one another. The barkeep's hands froze on the glass as his mustache twitched.

"The Corners boys owe me a fine bit. Now, if I was to go spreading their personal information around to strangers, they might not show up in my place again."

Sloan flicked the leather pouch again. A month's pay for him, but worth every penny if it got him enough facts to find the Corners' homestead tonight. The new sheriff didn't know and the land office wouldn't be open until ten the next morning. But even the sheriff couldn't force anyone to divulge the information. Sloan looked at the barkeep.

"Guess you'll have to decide if you want that bill paid or those boys back in here wanting more of your whiskey for free."

The barkeep was tempted. Sloan saw it in his eyes. But the man stiffened and went back to polishing his glass. "Maybe, maybe not. Fact is, Joseph was telling me that he's set to come into some money. I need customers that have a good income. There's nothing that says I need to like them any too much."

"What kind of money?" Sheriff Seth Kindle turned from where he'd been leaning against the bar to aim his gaze at the barkeep. "From where? What I hear is, that family hasn't worked their land in years. Knowing about a crime makes you guilty, too."

"I didn't admit to nothing, lawman."

Sloan wasn't in the mood to let the information slip out of his grip. Kindle was a lawman and that shiny badge pinned to his vest had a habit of shutting up men like the barkeep. "It's simple, really. I can cover the man's bill in exchange for information or you can deal with the sheriff tomorrow when we get that information from the land deed office. Either way, I'll get what I want. You'll be the one left with a bar tab and no one to make good on the debt. My offer expires when I leave."

Sloan didn't bother to voice the fact that Kindle's deputies were on their way to the land deed office's manager. But the man lived on a homestead a good two hours' ride outside town. In the dark it might just be impossible to find, even for an experienced trail man. Sloan felt his gut twisting with the possibilities of what Joseph Corners might be doing with Brianna out on his land. But no one in town knew where that parcel was, except the barkeep in front of him. The game held the highest stakes he'd ever gambled with, but he was going to win. Well after midnight now, the saloon crowd had thinned out. This was the third bar they'd searched looking for information on Joseph. Silver Peak didn't want for watering holes.

"Guess we aren't doing business." Sloan reached for the pouch, but the barkeep placed the glass over it. "Joseph's a loud man with whiskey in his belly. I only overheard him talking, but I hear a lot of nonsense in this bar. That don't mean I run to the sheriff with every bummed-out miner who's prone to plotting crazy stuff while his head's in a whiskey bottle. They sleep it off and go back to their claims. That's not a crime."

"True enough. But a woman's gone missing this time." Kindle glared at the man as a trickle of sweat ran down the side of his face. "I find her up at his place and I'm coming back for you. That's a promise."

"Now see here!"

Sloan felt his temper snap. He grabbed the front of the barkeep's vest and hauled the man up against the bar. His eyes bulged as the tips of his boots scrapped along the wooden plank floor.

"The only thing that is going to be seen is my fist coming towards your face. That's my woman out there in the night and no one steals from me. Tell me where that weasel lives and I'll pay his tab off as a thank you. Don't tell me and I'll watch you rot on a chain gang along with Joseph Corners for kidnapping."

"Fine... He just said he was getting married. I thought it was one of them mail-order brides. I figured the girl was coming with a dowry. Honest. I never knew nothing about no kidnapping! Not one word, swear it on my mother's soul."

Sloan tightened his grip on the man's shirt. "Where's the claim?"

The barkeep muttered out the directions and Sloan forced himself to release the man. He didn't want to. He needed to kill something. Craved the solid flesh-to-flesh contact that would make sure no one ever touched his woman again.

"Let's go, Sloan."

Sheriff Kindle was already heading towards the door. Sloan eyed the barkeep. "I'll be back if you sent us on a fool's errand."

The barkeep swallowed roughly before Sloan turned to follow the lawman into the freezing night. He heard the barkeep pick up the pouch. Sloan had never spent a month's pay so fast or so well. For the first time in his life, he recognized that money meant nothing compared to a woman.

His woman...and he was going to find her.

Kindle was already sitting in his saddle as Sloan mounted his own horse.

"You can't kill him."

Sloan gathered up the reins as he kicked his mount into action. White puffs appeared in front of the animals' mouths as they took off into the early morning hours.

"I mean it, McAlister. I'd have to hang you if you pulled a trigger in cold blood. Corners is a coward. You won't be getting a fight out of the man."

His blood wasn't cold, far from it. Rage flowed through him like a spring river gorged with melting snow.

"McAlister."

"I heard you, Kindle." Sloan didn't slow his mount. He shot a hard look at the lawman. "You get the first shot, but if he slips through your grasp I'm taking a shot. I'm not going to spend my life looking over my shoulder for that bastard."

"You might be wrong."

"Then I'll apologize." Kindle rolled his eyes at the idea. Sloan simply shrugged. "The only thing I'm wrong about was thinking Joseph had been put off back on the dock. I didn't finish the job. Brianna's up there or he knows where she is."

Jed reined his horse in closer to Sloan's. The night was half gone and darkness blanketed everything as the early morning hours crept by. "She's been up there a good amount of time."

Jed kept his voice low, but it sliced into Sloan like newly sharpened razor blades. He didn't like the sting, because nothing should matter so much to him. An iron-hard rule that Brianna had somehow managed to melt in two. Jed was right about one thing, she had been with Joseph Corners too long. One minute was too long. He tightened his grip on his rifle. It might be uncivilized, but he enjoyed the solid steel of the weapon resting against his palm. Always had. It allowed him to slip into a calm that could prove deadly to anyone who crossed him. Joseph had stepped way over the line.

"Let's go find her."

Warren and Jed moved in tight as the sheriff and his men led the way. They knew the road better and, in the dark, it was an advantage that Sloan needed. It would still be early morning before they reached the claim. The amount of time ate a hole in his gut. The idea of what he might find tormented him. He shoved it all aside, forcing his attention to the task of finding Brianna.

Finding Brianna alive was what mattered. He'd deal with the rest of it after he had her back in his arms.

Chapter Eight

Cold did funny things to the mind. Brianna didn't much mind at the moment though. She enjoyed the strange dreams of her life's moments and Christmas mornings from her past. But her stocking was empty. She pushed her hand down into it, searching for even one piece of sweetbread, but all she felt was the scratchy wool yarn the sock was made of. Her belly growled deep and long as slumber faded away in the face of hard hunger.

Her eyes fluttered open. The first rays of dawn were turning the cabin gray. Two of her captors were snoring louder than full-grown hogs. Her lips rose in a tiny smile at the image. Joseph did remind her of a hog. He was lazy enough to enjoy wallowing in filth. At least a hog had only a simple brain to excuse its lack of hygiene.

Her belly rumbled again as that smile made her lips hurt because the tender skin was dry. Thirst made her mouth feel like cotton as she rubbed her fingers against each other trying to warm them. She couldn't feel her toes hidden inside her shoes and her entire body shook as her knickers failed to keep the winter morning chill away.

At least the night was past. She focused her attention on the increasing light, trying to force her mind to think. The sun was rising and the temperature would increase now. She clung to that idea, actually fantasizing about the sun as it cleared the horizon, spreading its rays out to warm the air.

The bar across the front door splintered and flew to pieces. The door pushed back into the cabin with enough force to rip the top leather hinge out of the frame. The snoring ended as Joseph and his kin grumbled while trying to regain their wits. They didn't do it fast enough. The cabin was already full of black dusters. Polished rifles gleamed in the early morning light as they were pointed at the disoriented inhabitants.

"Brianna, move over this way."

Sloan's voice was deadly. Too calm and controlled, but it was the sweetest music she had ever heard. Lifting her hands from where she'd tucked them between her thighs the chains attached to her shackles rattled loudly. The cussing from Joseph and his family stopped instantly as the metal sound filled the cabin. Joseph pushed back away from the rifle in front of his chest, while his face turned pasty white. The shackles damned him instantly.

Sloan's eyes darkened as his gaze traced the chains. He turned his attention to the man standing in the doorway. "That enough proof for you, Sheriff?" The tone of his voice was even lower now and it sent a shiver through her. Sloan wasn't in the mood to be told no.

"Sure is." The lawman raised his rifle, aiming it at Joseph's father. "You went too far this time, Jonah. This here is illegal and I'm going to have to haul you and your boys into town."

"I'll tell you what's against the law. Breaking in a man's door. That's what's illegal!" Jonah raised his fist, but didn't move towards any of the muzzles aimed his way. "Besides, the boy done it. Stupid fool is in love. He's the one you need to take in."

"Pa!" Joseph's voice cracked as he whimpered for his father to protect him from his own transgressions. But the lack of moral fiber that ran through him clearly came from his father, because his sire and brothers all turned to point at him.

"Yeah, Joseph done it. Not me."

Sloan wasn't interested in the sniveling that filled the cabin. His finger itched to pull the trigger. He clamped down on the impulse as he aimed his attention at Joseph. The man trembled with fear. Sweat popped out on his forehead in spite of the cold.

"The key."

Joseph frowned. It was an ugly expression filled with hate. He spat on the floor as he pulled a brass key out of his vest pocket. Sloan stared right back with an equal amount of hatred. They stood facing off over her as Brianna felt her jaw drop open. Never once had she ever thought that she could inspire any man to fight for her. This morning it was a beautiful sight that sent a surge of excitement through her.

Sloan never took his eyes off Joseph. "Toss it to her and don't miss."

Joseph hesitated, his fingers turning white because he pressed so hard on the key. One dark eyebrow rose on Sloan's face before he lowered his head to look down the sights of his weapon.

"Do it, man." The sheriff wasn't in any better mood as he aimed his gun at Joseph. "I can't believe you left her chained up in this chill. You'll be lucky if the judge doesn't hang you for it."

The key clattered on the floor next to her feet. Joseph whimpered like a child, muttering words that didn't make any sense. She stared at the key for a long moment, held mesmerized by the fact that freedom was in reach. Her fingers reached for it just like the child in her dream had done looking for sweetbread. Her belly rumbled again as she tried to make her fingers work. The key clattered back to the floor, but she grabbed it and fit the end into one shackle. The heavy iron fell towards the wall as the chain rattled.

Just one short day she'd been locked in the iron bands, but the sweetest relief moved through her as she fit that key into the remaining shackle and turned it. Metal ground against metal and the rusty lock groaned before opening. She stumbled as she tried to stand, her legs too cold to work without wobbling. She fell against the wall and dug her fingers into the packed mud as she tried to summon enough willpower to make it out of the cabin.

Her face suddenly flamed as she realized she stood there in her knickers. Her temper flared and she cheerfully let it burn because it gave her the strength to stomp over to the pile of her ruined dress. Gathering it up, she hugged it against her open bodice.

"Move behind me, Brianna."

An insane impulse taunted her to lay a solid slap cross Joseph's face while she had the chance, but the cold fury in Sloan's voice held her hand. Her feet were already moving towards the cabin door when Joseph made a lunge for her. His fingers caught her tangled hair, gripping the delicate strands. He yanked on it and her body jerked towards his. Pain ripped through her body making her temper explode. The need to retaliate was too great. Lifting her foot she smashed it into Joseph's crotch. She stumbled right past him as he yelped and rolled onto his bunk. A hard hand gripped her arm and pulled her right off the floor as if she were a child.

"God damn it, Jonah. Why didn't you teach your boys any better?" Sheriff Kindle moved forward with his rifle still pointed at the Corners men. "This is turning into one hell of a mess. You are all going to have to sit in jail until the circuit judge comes 'round. I've seen too much to ignore."

She missed the remainder of the lawman's lecture because Sloan didn't let her go until she was outside the cabin. He blocked the doorway with his body, his shoulders filling it. But he kept his eyes on the sheriff as she heard the distinct sound of iron cuffs being locked into place. A shudder worked its way over her skin as she

150

realized that she was going to hear that iron grating sound in her dreams for the rest of her life.

Brianna shook off the chill as she wrapped her ruined petticoat around her shoulders like a cape. Her body quivered as she tried to keep her legs straight. Every muscle felt as limp as taffy. But she was determined to walk away from her jailers. No Spencer child was going to collapse because of a little chill and hunger. No sir!

As she lifted her face, a startled gasp left her lips. She found another pair of black eyes watching her. This pair belonged to an Indian. His hair was coal black and brushed his shoulders. Whatever he might be thinking, he masked it expertly. His gaze lingered on her for a long moment before he nodded with approval.

"You do not shriek. That is good."

She clutched her makeshift cape closer against the wind and scoffed at his comment. "Yelling sure isn't a lot of help to anyone."

"No, but keeping a rifle at hand is."

A chill raced down her back that had nothing to do with the snow. Jerking her head back towards the cabin, she stared into Sloan's eyes. Fury danced in his dark gaze, but she was still too glad to see him to truly worry about anything beyond the fact he was real. His temper didn't stand up to her stare. Emotion flickered in his gaze before he shook his head and surveyed her from tousled hair to frozen toes. A dangerous look invaded his expression as he reached out to trace the side of her face.

Even the gentle touch hurt. The bruises she knew would show up were right on time.

"It's nothing."

His gaze slid over the torn mess of her dress. Ripped edges of calico and muslin from her petticoat whipped around in the wind. She huddled under it, but her knickers and legs were in plain sight.

It was the most undignified position she'd ever experienced, but she was still so glad to see her rescuers that a grin decorated her abused lips.

"It sure as hell is something to me." Sloan smoothed a finger along her jaw.

The sheriff led Jonah out of his cabin by the chains attached to his wrists. Sloan's hand tightened on his rifle as she watched him fight off the urge to point the muzzle back at Jonah.

"She done said she loved my boy!"

The sheriff secured the chain to the back of his horse before the men waiting outside the cabin came forward to claim Joseph and his brothers.

"Save it, Corners. I saw the girl in shackles with my own eyes. That's about as far from love as it gets. It's a good thing the judge don't come 'round for another two weeks, cause I think you need the time to sort out your thoughts. You tell that crap to Ambrose and he just might consider giving you a taste of hard labor."

It was such a simple ending. Brianna watched the deputies pull Joseph and his brothers towards town. They walked their horses, forcing their prisoners to follow or be dragged. Joseph cussed as his younger brother whimpered. Fatigue suddenly rose up and slashed right into her. Her eyelids were so heavy, it hurt to keep them open. Every muscle she owned began to shake. Her legs felt like butter, too soft to support her weight.

Sloan moved before her brain grasped that he was in motion. A hard arm snaked around her waist as he clasped her to his larger frame. He handed off his rifle to the Indian before hooking her knees and lifting her up. Her body shook harder as her fingers dug into the harsh fabric of his black duster. She caught a hint of his scent and it drew a long sigh from her lips. It was a tiny sound that only reached his ears, but she saw the corners of his lips twitch slightly in response. Maybe she was only seeing what she wanted to, but for the moment it was perfection.

CR

Her belly refused to let her sleep very long. It rumbled and hurt as it cramped up. Rolling over, Brianna gasped as pain twisted through her middle making her eyes sting with unshed tears. Her nose caught the full aroma of cooking food and another cramp twisted her gut. Staring across the room to her little stove, she blinked at the sight of Sloan tending to whatever was cooking in her iron pot. His black duster was missing, but his rifle leaned against the wall within easy reach. He was wearing only a shirt today, no over-vest to complicate his appearance by making the man look too formal. His shirtsleeves were rolled up, displaying his forearms. Coupled with the fact that the door was firmly closed and she was still in her corset and knickers, the moment was far too intimate.

"That bastard didn't feed you, did he?"

Sitting up, Brianna felt her mouth water just because they were talking about food. "No."

Sloan picked up a plate and began spooning up whatever he'd cooked. She didn't care what it was, as long as it was food. Mule meat would have found favor at the moment. Steam rose from the pile of beans. She detected the scent of bacon mixed in, too. A westerner's staple, the beans absorbed the salt and fat from the bacon. The local Indians called it "chili" and often put other vegetables or different meats into the mix.

Brianna held out her hands for the food. The spoon resting on the side of the tin plate rattled because her body shook. The tremor running down her limbs made her mad. "Joseph thought he could starve me into a wedding."

She placed a spoonful of the meal into her mouth to avoid mentioning any details beyond Joseph's main goal. The memory of his bare cock made her thighs squeeze tight as she took another bite.

Sloan's eyes caught the defensive motion. His lips pressed into a hard line as he watched her clean the plate. She was too hungry to care how ungraceful it was to shovel the steaming food into her mouth like a miner. Her brain urged her to eat as fast as possible in spite of the fact that she understood the ordeal was over. She scraped the last bit of food off the plate and swallowed it with a satisfied sigh.

"What did he want in exchange for some warmth?"

She choked. Her eyes rounded as her memory offered up a perfect recollection of just what Joseph wanted to demand from her. Her temper ignited as she felt a spike of terror go through her. Joseph Corners certainly wasn't worth her fear!

"It doesn't matter, because he'll never get it from me." She stood and moved across the floor to place the empty plate on the sideboard where her sink was. A tin of water was standing in her sink and she plunged her hands into it. She suddenly felt filthy.

"I need a bath." She didn't care if her voice sounded desperate or not. Her skin felt like it was crawling with vermin.

"I figured you'd say that."

Her large pot was steaming on the back burner of the stove. The white vapor looked like heaven to her. The bedroom door was open and her tub shimmered like an oasis.

She didn't give Sloan another thought. Ripping at her few remaining garments, she didn't even wait for him to add the hot water. The need to scrub her skin didn't care if the water was one degree above freezing. She stepped into the cold water and sat down as he poured the steaming water in.

"Slow down, honey." His voice was low, but so sweet she felt tears sting her eyes. Her emotions teetered dangerously as she tried to cling to her composure. It seemed a poor ending to dissolve into a weeping puddle now that she was back under her own roof, but her fickle feelings wanted to take center ring. Cupping her hands under the water, she drenched her face to avoid letting Sloan see the tears glistening in her eyes.

Her soap bar appeared in his hand as he held it up for her. Grabbing it, she attacked her legs and body with a zeal that left her skin pink. His hand invaded her bath as it captured her wrist. He pulled the soap from her grasp, while his opposite hand pushed her shoulders gently forward.

"It's over." He moved the soap over her shoulder blades in a soothing motion.

"I know." She did but her body quivered as he washed her like a newborn. It didn't make any sense, but it felt so secure that she closed her eyes to savor the moment. She didn't want to think about what might happen tomorrow, all that mattered was that Sloan was here now.

He rinsed her off and she stood. Uncaring of the fact that she was nude. Confidence filled her as she watched the way his obsidian eyes traced her curves. She felt beautiful, so completely radiant in that moment. There were no words to describe it because she witnessed it on his face.

Her lover's face.

Her nipples tingled before drawing into tight little buttons. His gaze lowered to her chest, watching them peak. Sloan reached for her arm and his fingers curled around her biceps. Their eyes met and a ripple of sensation shook her as she witnessed the fury burning in those dark orbs.

"Take me to bed." Her voice was husky. A blush warmed her face, but she didn't look away from her companion. A solid tug and she tumbled into his chest. He slid his arm around her waist to press her against his frame. "Joseph isn't the only man around here who'll covet this mill or your body."

"I know." She pressed her fingers against his disapproving frown, tracing his lower lip with a fingertip. "Let's talk about it later."

Temptation flickered in his eyes. She felt his chest shudder with a rough breath as he slipped one hand down her back. He clasped a cheek in a firm hand, gently squeezing as he watched her. She felt the unmistakable bulge of his erection against her belly. Hot need bubbled up inside her with frightening speed. Her hands curled into talons that clawed at his shirt-covered chest. A frantic need ran through her to share her body with the man of her choice. All her life, she'd been lectured on keeping her purity, but today it felt far more important to be in charge of just who she gave her favors to. The cold and hunger would have broken her at some point, because the instinct to live was stronger. It was a harsh fact that made her stretch up to Sloan's firm mouth.

"Kiss me." She smiled at the sound of her order. It echoed through her thoughts, driving Joseph's sniveling demands out.

He met her halfway, his lips pressing a hard kiss against hers. Twisting in his embrace, she kissed him back with all the raw emotion pouring out of her. Her fingers pulled on his shirt, searching for his skin. She reached between them to stroke his cock through his britches. A soft snarl of achievement broke through their kiss as she handled his sex because she wanted to. Not because he'd ordered her to do it.

Joseph's words rose in her head and she greedily let her hands begin to act out his demands on the man of her choice. Fallen woman maybe, but at least she wasn't a frightened little virgin anymore. Childhood needed to end sometime.

Brianna groaned as he broke off their kiss. Sloan frowned at her as he fingered her jaw.

"Does it hurt?" Desire made his tone rough. It unleashed more excitement inside her, touching off a deep yearning to toss everything civilized aside. She wanted to be used by him and meet him in the middle of that battleground where she could take as well as be taken.

"I want you naked too, Sloan."

Taking a half-step away from him, she watched his reaction to her boldness.

Speaking the command aloud excited her. A harsh grunt came from Sloan as his lips twitched up.

"All right, honey, we'll do it your way." His eyes glittered with passion as he crooked one finger in her direction. "I enjoy your hands on me a whole lot."

Closing the distance between them, she rubbed over the front of his chest as she searched for the buttons holding his shirt closed. He sucked in a breath and waited as she opened each one, trailing a single fingertip over his bare skin. The hair covering his hard chest was dark and crisp. She enjoyed his hardness just as much as he liked her curves. It delighted her because it was such a contrast to the softness of her own body.

"Don't forget the pants."

His voice hinted at a dare. She licked her lower lip as need burned hotter inside her. She never hesitated, but popped open his waistband when she reached where his shirt was tucked into his pants. The smaller buttons that secured his fly didn't take long to unfasten and she boldly let her fingertips stroke the hard flesh of his cock. His cheek flinched as a groan escaped his lips. Hunger glittered in his eyes as she reached completely into his pants to close her fingers around his length.

"Does it help to be in control?"

"Yes," she almost shouted. He chuckled at her, cupping her face and smoothing his fingers over the tender spots left by the blows she'd received. Her eyes closed as his fingers moved over the same skin that had been abused. Sloan's touch was a healing balm that soaked into her soul, restoring her balance.

"That's it, honey. Don't let anyone keep you under their heel." He laid a soft kiss on top of one bruise. His lips trailed a string of tender salutations over her jaw and up her cheek. A shudder shook her body as her breath rattled roughly from her chest. The tension melted away as his cock twitched in her grasp.

She needed to test out another one of Joseph's demands before she let Sloan claim her body again. She had no idea where the urge came from, only that she was determined to prove she would perform when she wanted to and not because she was broken into submission.

Lowering to her knees, she pulled his cock into view. The head was as thick as a plum with a slit on its top. A ridge of flesh ran around the top of it. Leaning forward, she let her tongue lap that slit.

"Holy Christ! That bastard wanted you to suck him off?"

A hard hand gripped her hair to hold her head away from his cock. He controlled the grip, preventing pain from shooting through her scalp. Raising her gaze, she looked at the harsh anger on his face, but it was overshadowed by excitement.

"So what? I wouldn't do it, but I want to try it now with you."

A husky chuckle was his response. Admiration flickered in his eyes as he released her hair. "All right, honey. Flex your wings."

Leaning forward, she let her mouth open enough to fit around the head. One hand was still threaded through her hair and it flexed as she closed her lips around his cock. A harsh grunt hit her ears, kicking up her desire as the power shifted between them again. She was the one on her knees, but the control rested with her. Trailing her fingers over his length she let her tongue play with the part that was inside her mouth. The scent of his skin filled her senses as she pulled her head away and opened her jaw wider to take more of his length. The hand in her hair flexed again as a growl rose from his chest. A sound of deep enjoyment that made her even more determined to keep at the task. His hips jerked forward as a muffled word got caught between his clenched teeth.

He pulled her head away. Brianna raised her face to look at his and shivered at the expression. She'd pushed him past his limit this time. There was no more patience, only hard hunger dancing in his dark eyes.

"I need to get inside you."

It was the sweetest compliment she'd ever heard. The naked honesty made her shake with need. It didn't make sense and she didn't want it to. Her skin was rosy-warm and she just longed to be free of every stitch.

Sloan clasped his hands around her waist and raised her off her knees, his gaze focused on her breasts. His grip tightened as he leaned down and sucked one hard nipple into his mouth. A sigh rose from her lips as he worried the sensitive tip with his tongue. He smoothed his fingers over the curves of her hips. He released her nipple and clasped each of her thighs.

"I just can't wait any longer, honey." He picked her up and moved between her thighs. Pushing them wide with his hips. He pressed her against the wall as the head of his cock nudged the folds of her sex.

"Hold onto my shoulders."

There was hard demand in his voice. It excited her, making that spot at the top of her sex throb with anticipation. Her body felt empty to the point of desperation. Her hips tilted towards him as she wrapped her arms around his neck. He pressed his entire chest against hers, the hair rasping against her smooth skin. His hips drove his cock up into her with a smooth motion that made her whimper.

"I've never wanted to be inside a woman so damn much in my life."

He pulled free and pushed deeper. Pleasure filled her as she tried to move her hips in time with his, but he held her hard against the wall. There was only delight as he gripped her bottom and thrust between her thighs. Sensation took command of her thoughts, jerking her away from anything beyond meeting the pace her partner set. Her heart pounded as it sent blood racing through her veins. Every inch of her skin was acutely sensitive and it heightened every point of contact between their bodies. But the deepest sensation was centered around his cock. Deep inside her, it twisted and tightened as she tried to push her hips against him harder, but was held in place for his desire.

The hands on her bottom tightened and a hard rasp rattled through his clenched teeth. There was no control in either of them and she let the moment drag her down with him. Pleasure broke through her as she felt the spurt of his release. It crashed into her womb, shaking her like a leaf in a stormy wind. She clung tighter to her lover as her lips couldn't contain the moan of delight that rose from her. It mixed with the harsh, male sound of enjoyment shaking him as she clung to him.

"Was I too rough?"

Her face burned. Brianna marveled at her body, because she sure didn't understand why a question was any cause for blushing when she was still impaled on his cock with a wall against her back.

"Look at me."

Command was back in his voice. Her eyelashes fluttered as she tried to look at him, but felt her blush deepen instead. A soft chuckle shook him and she raised her face to investigate the change in his mood. A firm kiss landed on her mouth before he lifted her free and set her feet on the floor.

"Talking to your partner is one of the best parts of having a lover."

Brianna felt her eyes widen. Talk? About sex? Now that was certainly something she had never dared to fantasize about. People simply did not do that. At least not decent folks.

Sloan turned and swiped her knickers off the floor. He held them out to her as his expression went blank again. Determination flickered in his eyes once more and she recognized it now. Sloan was about to demand his way with her.

"Get dressed. We'll practice pillow talk after we go into town."

With her heart slowed down, she felt the chill in the air. Shaking her head, she moved towards her dresser. "I need clean ones." Picking up her ruined bodice from the floor she frowned at the waste.

"Put on a Sunday dress." Sloan was working the buttons on his fly closed. He only gave her a firm glance when she lifted an eyebrow at his direction.

"You'll need to sign a complaint at the sheriff's office."

His gaze dropped down her nude length, making her shiver as she realized how vulnerable she was to him. It didn't seem very fair that nature could simply rear her head one moment and sweep aside her good intentions. Sloan McAlister tempted her beyond her resolve to remain on the straight and narrow path. But it happened every time she was alone with him. Every scrap of self-control she owned deserted her in a flash. The only thing that made it bearable was the evidence that she affected him in a similar fashion.

"Why a Sunday dress? Sheriff Kindle isn't that important to my way of thinking."

His eyes rose back up her body, hesitating at her breasts before locking stares with her once again. Solid determination blazed at her, tempered with anticipation.

"As much as I'm glad to hear that, put the dress on for me. We're going to stop at the church and get married."

Chapter Nine

"I sure don't need any man marrying me because he feels sorry for me being alone." The words crossed her lips before she thought about them. Gaining a husband through pity felt worse than being broken by hunger to warm Joseph's bed.

A low sound of amusement came from Sloan. But there was nothing pleasant about it. He moved across the floor without a sound and cupped her chin in his hand. "Trust me, honey, pity isn't on the list of reasons why we're going to see the good parson." His lips pressed into a hard line before she felt his opposite hand cup one bare breast.

"I'm going to spend tonight, and tomorrow night, and every night after that between your thighs. So, unless you want the gossips in town counting up the months between your wedding and the birth of our baby, get that dress on before I climb back on top of you."

"I never thought about a baby..." Fear traced a path through her head for the first time.

She'd never considered anything but herself. Horror flooded her as Brianna choked on the possible reality of a tiny little life growing inside her. Oh, she sure was stupid at times. There were a lot of things that might be overlooked in the West, but "bastard" was still a harsh title for a kid to shoulder. Making her own choices was one thing, branding someone else with the title of illegitimate was quite another.

"Considering how we affect each other, I'd suggest you get dressed for your wedding. Now."

He released her chin and moved towards the door. Brianna watched him reach for his vest and shrug into it. "But we don't know each other."

A wicked grin lifted his lips as his eyes roamed over her nude body again. "We know a lot more than some couples. The rest can come along. But no child of mine is going to be born without a name." His eyes flashed at her as he buttoned up his vest. "Get into that dress, honey, before your sweet little nipples tempt me past any good intentions."

Brianna felt a lump form in her throat. He did feel sorry for her. Regret could make a person do a lot of things, but she sure didn't like the idea of Sloan marrying her because of some misplaced guilt over taking her virginity. Letting a chemise drop over her head, she blinked back the two tears stinging her eyes.

"You don't have to marry me, Sloan. You didn't seduce me." It was by far one of the hardest things she'd ever said. But he was worth the effort, even if it meant that she was handing him permission to walk out of her door forever. A twist of pain went through her at just the idea. So sharp she almost moaned out loud. Her pride held the sound back, because she didn't want him if he didn't *want* to be standing beside her. A lot of folks said plenty of stuff in church that they never practiced at home. Even if she did find herself with child, better an honest bastard than a deserted unwanted wife.

That grin lifted his lips once more as he crossed back to where she stood. A hard arm encircled her waist, pulling her against his body. She shivered as she realized how slight she was compared to him. The grin actually lit up his eyes for a change, making her heart light.

"No, I didn't seduce you. For the record, I don't want your father's mill. But having a husband will put an end to every out-of-luck mongrel that does want it." The grin faded as hunger took command of his gaze. "That's just an excuse though. I want you, honey, and I'm going to spend the night deep inside you. I did have a mother once who taught me a manner or two. So, we are going to get married before I take you back to bed."

His eyes flashed a warning at her that made her body surge with renewed heat. His hand clasped one side of her bottom, pressing her against the bulge of his cock. It was already hard again and her mouth went dry as she stared at the face of a man who wasn't going to forget what he'd just promised her. In all honesty, she loved the idea.

"All right."

CR

Warren surveyed her in silence as they waited in the church aisle. Jed, the half-breed, was along as well, waiting to serve as witness to her wedding. Her intended husband introduced both men while Brianna plucked at her blue calico skirt with nervous fingers. Somehow, the fact that everyone in town was about to know Sloan was warming her bed made her jumpy. Her curious mind poked at that little bit of information. Why was sex so unspeakable? Everyone sure was happy to see new babies baptized on Sunday morning.

Reverend Pilkerton enjoyed any reason to put on his black preacher's robe. His wife was ruby cheeked as she fussed with the back of it to make sure it was straight across his shoulders. Their eight children lined up to watch the bustle, the oldest daughter holding the hand of the youngest child. She flashed Brianna a sweet smile that looked a little misplaced because she was still wearing a dress meant for a girl when her face had blossomed into a lovely young woman. She gazed longingly at Sloan while her father turned to face the bride-to-be.

"Well now, my children. Are you sure you've considered entering into holy matrimony with proper respect for the Almighty?"

The reverend rolled the word "holy" taking three times as long to say it as he needed. A gleam twinkled in his eye as his wife handed him a large Bible. He ran loving fingers over the worn edges before opening it. He paused for a moment and looked at Brianna, his smile fading.

"Is there any news of your father?"

Brianna straightened her spine. Firm belief in her father's good heath still remained in her heart. "No, sir, but I'm certain there's a good reason for his absence."

The reverend transferred his harsh glare to Sloan. "I don't recall your face among the congregation, son."

Only a man of the cloth could get away with labeling Sloan "son". Brianna fought to control a smile before it got the reverend's attention back on her.

"No, sir, you haven't." Sloan shrugged his overcoat aside to display his badge. "The lawless don't respect the Sabbath."

"A sad truth." Every one of the reverend's children nodded in unison with their parents. The girls' pigtails bobbed along with their chins. A large smile appeared on the reverend's face. "Well, I'm happy to see you respecting the Lord's law. Very happy indeed to see you standing in front of the altar. Marriage is a ho—ly estate, you know."

Brianna felt a lump swell up in her throat. Her eyes locked onto the big black Bible as she felt her collar bite into her neck. Maybe she'd always accepted the idea that one day she'd marry, but today she felt her heart race as she faced the reverend. The row of grinning faces behind the altar captured her attention. Sloan really did have the right idea. Children needed the good favor of the town. She'd made the choice to share her body with a man, but it would be the fruit of that labor that bore the stain if she refused to wed her lover.

A large hand spread wide on her lower back. It was such a tender touch that she shifted her eyes to look at the man becoming her lawfully wedded husband. His fingers rubbed gently across her hips as the reverend's voice bounced off the back wall of the church.

Twenty minutes later, they were married. Sloan turned her towards the door as the Pilkerton family offered a round of applause. The reverend slid the five-dollar gold piece Sloan offered him beneath his robe and into a front vest pocket for safekeeping. She stepped into the evening gray and gasped as Warren swept her up against his chest.

"Got to kiss the bride." His mouth pressed against hers in a far more passionate kiss than she'd ever witnessed at any wedding. Jed stole her from him before she regained enough sense to push him away. A low rumble escaped Sloan's mouth as he glared at his friends. Twin smirks appeared on their faces before she watched them shoulder their rifles as devotedly as any mother handling her babe. The guns had been left in the coat rack for the ceremony, but they served as a harsh reminder that Silver Peak didn't respect Christian values a lot of times.

"Time to see the sheriff."

There was a note of firm enjoyment in Sloan's voice. Glancing at her groom, Brianna shivered. Possessiveness tightened his features as he stared at her. She suddenly felt like his next meal, the promise he'd made back at her cabin to spend the night inside her echoing through her skull.

Sheriff Kindle was cradling a steaming mug of coffee when they arrived. He looked harassed as Joseph and his father started yelling the moment they recognized who had come into the jailhouse.

"I told you to be quiet. There ain't nothing you can say that will change what I witnessed with my own eyes. You're staying behind bars until Ambrose ships you off to the quarry for hard labor. There's no room in Silver Peak for kidnappers of women. Not while I wear this badge."

The sheriff touched the brim of his hat in respect before he ground his teeth with frustration over the whining from his prisoners.

"Go ahead and let them loose."

Brianna stared at her new husband in shock. Sloan had turned so that his voice made it into the cells Joseph and his kin occupied. Silence instantly fell over them as he fingered the trigger of his rifle. The weapon still lay against his shoulder, but the slight motion of his finger, gliding over the trigger, was unmistakable.

"My apologies, Kindle. Forgot to mention that Miss Spencer did me the honor of becoming my wife a few minutes ago." Sloan never took his eyes off Joseph as he spoke. The sheriff's chair skidded backwards as he stood.

"Is that a fact?"

Sloan turned his attention to the lawman and leveled the same hard stare at him. "It is. The good reverend was real pleased to see me respecting the holy teachings."

"I bet." Kindle aimed his gaze at her. "Sure you like that promise you just made in church, ma'am? It can be annulled."

Her respect for the sheriff suddenly tripled. He stood firm in the face of Sloan's displeasure, ready to place himself between them if she breathed a single word of protest. Her pride didn't care for the battle being waged over her father's property, but she still valued the stand the lawman was willing to take to ensure that she wasn't being strong-armed into a marriage.

"I find myself quite fortunate to have so devoted a husband."

Kindle shook his head. "He's firm in his actions, all right. But it could still be annulled."

A little stain of heat touched her face as she recognized that Sloan had already consummated their vows. She'd enjoyed it, too, so marching off to the church to plead for an annulment was rather dishonest. She might be a slave to lust now, but she wasn't a liar. She shook her head and watched Sloan's lips twitch. He never let the smile show, but she caught the glimmer of enjoyment in his eyes. It sent a bolt of heat through her. It tempted her to suspect there was more than lust driving his decision to wed her. Oh, it might be a foolish daydream, but she hugged the idea close and refused to think about annulments. She was going to enjoy her wedding night.

"Thank you, Sheriff Kindle. However, I am very content with my promise before the reverend. I trust you will recall that if anything unfortunate happens to myself or my new husband?"

Kindle glared at Sloan before inclining his head towards her. "Yes, ma'am, my memory is real good."

Joseph let out a curse that turned her face red. Sloan stared at the sorry excuse for a boy stuck in a man's body. His father had allowed him to strangle on his own selfishness. Children didn't achieve without a parent expecting it of them. Silver Peak was full of lazy men who flooded the area looking for an easy life.

"You won't find stealing from me so simple, Corners. Keep your hands off my wife."

Joseph actually stepped away from the cell door that he was holding onto. He sputtered as he recognized his own cowardice. Sloan stroked his rifle once more before turning his full attention back to the sheriff.

"If you'll excuse us, it's our wedding night."

Brianna resisted her husband's pull. With a gentle hand, she unhooked his fingers from her arm and moved towards the cells where Joseph stood fuming at her. She forced herself to look at him. He spat on the floor in front of her and a smile lifted the corners of her lips.

"My husband is correct, it is our wedding night. I do hope you enjoy it as much as we shall."

She caught a low snicker from Kindle before she turned and joined Sloan. A gleam of appreciation twinkled in his eyes as she rested her hand on his forearm and proudly stepped out into the sunlight. News of their wedding traveled fast and shop owners waved as they walked down the plank boardwalk.

"Congratulation, Brianna."

"Be happy, dear!"

"Your father would be proud."

He would be. Brianna waved back as she tightened her hold on her husband. Yes, she did believe that her daddy would approve.

Sloan leaned down close to her ear. "Just think, they all know exactly what we're planning to do when we get back to your place."

Her face turned scarlet as she glared at him. Sloan's lips twitched with amusement as she sputtered and blushed some more.

"Sloan McAlister, you're incorrigible."

He growled softly for her hearing alone. "And you love it, hard and fast."

Heat hit her and consumed every inch of her body. She was suddenly in a rush to get home as that spot at the top of her sex throbbed. Her knickers bothered her when she looked into the eyes of her husband and felt her mouth go dry. Hunger, raw and uncontrolled, blazed back at her.

Chapter Ten

His new wife blushed all the way back to her cabin. He should have felt guilty for annoying her but the flat truth was...he didn't. Brianna cast him a furious look the moment Warren and Jed bid her good night. Her hips swayed and sent her petticoat swishing away from her ankles as her temper fired her step.

"You did that on purpose, Sloan McAlister."

Her new husband didn't answer, but moved across the floor to stand his rifle against the wall next to the bed. Her throat tightened as she recognized the significance of the placement of his weapon. But she still propped her hands onto her hips as he turned back to face her.

"That's right, I did." He shrugged out of his duster and laid it over the back of a chair. Her throat grew tighter as she watched his fingers begin to unbutton his vest. "Marriage means a whole lot of things to different folks. To me, it means I can stop trying to avoid every single impulse you inspire in me."

"I see." It was an odd compliment. One that she had never considered before, but it sounded so completely right. Sloan wasn't some example of gentlemanly idealism. In truth, she didn't want him to be. It was his hardness she craved, not a chaste kiss on the back of her hand.

He folded his vest and placed it on top of his duster. A soft chuckle filled the cabin as he moved towards the stove. He pulled the front cooking plate up and dropped a scoop of new coal into the belly. A few turns from the poker and he replaced the plate as the coal sparked and began to burn, filling the room with more heat.

His gaze was as hot as the fire. He closed the distance between them as her temper died in a flash of passion. Her body didn't even heat up in slow degrees. It burst into clamoring need as he grasped her hips. A gasp rose from her lips at the pure carnal nature of the touch. It was bold and blunt, setting off a throbbing at the top of her sex.

"I've never been a rich man, until you let me into your bed." He pulled her forward so that she felt the outline of his erection. "Now I'm addicted to the good life."

His mouth pressed against hers in a firm kiss. He ran his tongue over her lower lip, teasing the tender skin until she opened her mouth to allow a deeper kiss. His tongue stroked down along her own as his hips thrust his cock against her belly. She was so aware of how empty her passage was. Her tongue tangled with his, mimicking his motions as sweet sensation flowed down to her sex. She stroked his chest, searching out the buttons on his shirt from memory now and pushing them through their holes to free him from the fabric. She actually hated the shirt and her dress at that moment. They were barriers that prevented her feeling his skin against hers.

His mouth left hers and trailed over her cheek. He captured the back of her head, the fingers threading up into her braided bun. He placed a soft kiss on the tender column of her neck before scraping over the same spot with his teeth. Excitement raced down her spine as she held her breath, waiting for him to bite her. It was an insane idea, but one that made her skin leap with awareness.

She gasped when he nipped her skin. Her nipples contracted beneath her corset, the hard tips complaining bitterly about being laced down. Another soft chuckle shook his chest. He raised his head to lock stares with her. His fingers searched through her hair, tugging out the pins that held it secure. He set them aside before combing her hair with his fingers, drawing it down in a soft curtain of brown silk.

"Take your dress off." He released her and took one short step away. His eyes burned with need as he raked her from head to toe. "Take everything off."

"I see the orders have begun." She pushed her lip out into a pout, but couldn't hold the expression for long. Fingering the button at her collar, she let the urge to play override her shyness. There was no place for timidity between them. Working the button, she watched the way his gaze followed her fingers to the next button and the one below it.

"I've got a few more demands to lay on you, wife."

Letting her bodice slip down her arms, she reached for her waistband. "Hmm...well, I suppose I might try to please you or I could simply be naughty and refuse your demands. Not all wives are obedient. I hear that some even have that part of the wedding ceremony omitted. They only vow to love, honor and respect but not obey."

She whirled around, showing him her back. She looked over her shoulder and winked at him.

"Either way, I owe you a few smacks on your fanny for leaving the rifle up here anyway."

She gasped and turned back around. His gaze instantly dropped to the swells of her breasts at the top of her corset. "I am not a child."

"Oh, I've noticed that sure enough. But you will listen to me when it comes to your safety, Brianna. I think you scared me half to death."

The deep tone of his voice made her shake with anticipation of just what he planned to do with her. Her skirt and petticoat fell to the floor and she stepped out of them. He shrugged out of his shirt at the same time and reached for his fly. Her lower lip went dry as her eyes focused on his fingers while they separated the front of his trousers. He sat down and pulled his boots off with a swift motion. When he stood back up, his pants were pushed down his legs with a quick motion. He clicked his tongue at her as one dark eyebrow rose.

"Ah, sweet wife, you've fallen behind." He waved a single finger back and forth in reprimand. "Maybe you're asking for that spanking. Some women enjoy it."

"Nonsense." She unbuttoned her waist tape and let her knickers drop down her thighs. His gaze feasted on her mons through the thin cotton of her chemise. She was nervous as she tried to decide if she was pretty or not. She wanted to be attractive to him, but had never really thought about her body one way or another.

"Some women say the marriage bed isn't enjoyable." His gaze rose to her face as she sat down and removed her shoes and stockings. "That's what I call nonsense or a selfish man." He brushed a hand through her hair again, letting his fingers filter through the threads.

It sounded more like a tragedy. She licked her lower lip as she considered never knowing what it felt like to enjoy the way their flesh connected. To think a majority of women wouldn't even believe her if she dared voice her newfound knowledge stunned her. She felt like a child with a secret so grand, it almost burst through her attempts to clamp it all inside her.

She dropped her corset and reached for the hem of her chemise. Lifting the final veil caused her hands to shake. She wasn't sure why, only that pleasing him was important to her. As the cotton cleared her head, she found his gaze stroking her nude frame in slow sweeps. No flattering phrase fit the moment. She saw her beauty etched on his face.

Sloan's gaze traveled down her bare frame, missing not even a single detail before returning to her face. "Come here, wife."

Her husband's voice was as thick as warm syrup. The words just as tempting. He pushed her onto her back as he leaned on one elbow alongside her. He cupped one breast, brushing the nipple with his thumb while his dark eyes watched.

"Pillow talk is vital between lovers." He pinched her nipple. A little jolt of sensation raced through her spine to that spot on the top of her sex. "Communication makes it so much more fun to go about consummating a marriage."

Brianna gasped. "Don't be wicked!" Her voice was a breathless whisper as his hand cupped her other breast and she waited for him to pinch that nipple as well.

"What's wicked about plain talking?" Her nipple begged for a pinch, but he only moved his fingers around the plump flesh of her breast.

"Talking about...um...marriage matters is wicked."

His eyebrow rose. "I don't think so. Might be naughty though." His hand left her breast and brushed down the center of her body. He paused just above the entrance to her sex. That spot hidden within the folds throbbed for attention as her face turned red from just the idea of being touched so intimately.

"If you don't tell me what you like, how do I know where to touch you next?" His fingers fanned out over her belly, one traveling into the curls on her mons but not quite far enough to stroke that little pulsing point. Her body twisted with anticipation, but Sloan trapped one of her legs with his and leaned over her torso to pin it to the bed. The rope creaked beneath them as he hovered just above her lips.

"Should I stroke your clit again? Or lick it?"

181

"Don't be absurd! No one does that." Oh, but her face turned beet red as she thought about it.

"Want to bet?"

She bucked up off the bed and he pressed her back down, leaning enough of his weight on her to lock her against the mattress. His finger pushed between the folds of her slit to find that throbbing spot. Her hips jerked as he rubbed it and pleasure shot deep into her passage.

"I'm not much of a gambling man, but why not? You sucked my cock. Lovers return the favor." His finger rubbed over her clit making sweat bead on her forehead as she struggled to breathe through her shock. His black eyes watched her as his finger continued to move on that sensitive spot. "Becoming your husband was a way of ensuring that I can remain your lover."

"Sloan..."

She never finished her protest. It died in a harsh gasp as he moved down the bed and right between her thighs. He pressed each leg up towards her waist and spread her wide. His breath brushed her wet slit a moment before she felt his tongue lap right up the center of her sex. He paused at the front where her clit throbbed for attention. His lips closed around the sensitive little bud, sucking it into his mouth. He spread the folds of her sex apart, keeping them away from that little button as he plied his tongue over it.

Pleasure bit into her so hard she shook with it. He used the tip of his tongue to rub it while he added the motion of sucking around it. Her hips bucked up towards his mouth, demanding harder strokes of his tongue. Her nipples hardened to the point where they almost hurt as her body jerked and pleasure ripped into her. Everything spun in a kaleidoscope of colors while the sound of her pounding heart filled her head. There was nothing but the spiral of pleasure turning her around and around until she collapsed back onto the bed, gasping for breath because she had forgotten to breathe.

"Now that is exactly why pillow talk is so much fun. I can't wait to hear you ask me to lap you again."

Her lips were frozen as she glanced down her body to where Sloan still hovered over her spread thighs. All thought deserted her as she watched him rise up over her. His cock was fully erect as he placed his hands on either side of her. His face was lit with conquest as he pressed his cock into her. Her passage stretched around his length as a ripple of delight went through her. It wasn't tight or demanding, instead it was a deep enjoyment of being filled. Sloan lowered his chest until the hair on his torso teased every inch of her breasts. His hips moved in a steady motion, driving his cock in and out of her body. She moaned softly as her body told her how much she enjoyed his hardness. Her hands curled around his arms, stroking the firm muscle that allowed him to lift her so easily. He leaned enough weight on her to hold her in place as her passage was filled with even more hard flesh.

"Tell me to move faster, honey."

He wasn't asking her, but ordering her to comply with his demand. Her eyes opened as her hips lifted to take his next thrust. Nothing mattered but the pleasure building beneath his thrusts. She shook with each deep penetration. The sensation tightened deeper in her belly this time and she surged up off the bed to force his cock to touch the bubble of pleasure in the center of her womb.

"Yes, faster. I want you to move faster now."

A harsh growl filled her ear as she dug her fingers into his arms. The bed rocked faster as that pleasure twisted through her once more. This time she yelled out loud because it was so intense. Sloan's body pressed her down into the mattress as he forced every last bit of his length into her passage. His cock jerked as he snarled and she felt his release deep inside her belly. The bed slowly stopped rocking as they both tried to regain their breath. The hard body above her shook as his chest worked to supply his heart. He rolled right over one shoulder and took her along with him. Their legs tangled as her head ended up on one side of his chest. He stroked her bare shoulder and the curve of her hip as the sound of his heart filled her head.

Sloan listened to his wife as she fell asleep. He was wide awake but happy to be aware of the moment. There was no greater delight than listening to her little mutters as she tried to wiggle away from him. He smoothed her back against his body and waited while she, unconscious, grew used to his presence in her bed. He reached up and turned down the wick in the lamp. The stove cast a red glow over the cabin. The wind rattled the door slightly, but he was suddenly more comfortable than he could ever recall being since that magical time when he was a boy who trusted his parents completely.

It felt like a mighty long time ago.

Reaching for a quilt, he flung it over his wife and enjoyed the knowledge that she was his. Maybe he didn't understand his reasons completely, but there was no mistaking the surge of enjoyment he got every time the word "wife" moved through his thoughts.

His...

Someway...somehow, he was in the one place he'd decided to avoid, but he sure was enjoying it. His wife was going to have to get used to him, because he wasn't leaving.

Chapter Eleven

At sunrise, Sloan was missing from her bed. Brianna stretched and winced at the soreness between her thighs. Her eyes stung, but she rubbed them and forced her body out of the bed. The falling snow wasn't going to provide her with much daylight to get her chores finished. Conserving her resources was now doubly important since being robbed, and that included the oil in the lamp. Work by day, sleep at night.

The front door stood unbarred and Sloan's rifle was missing. A moment of panic hit her as she realized he just might be gone. It twisted through her heart so acutely, she felt tears sting her eyes.

She was insane. A foolish girl in love.

Her eyes rounded as she recognized her own folly. Somewhere along the line she really had gone and jumped off that cliff that saw her plummeting towards complete loss of control when it came to her heart. There was no talking herself out of it. The emotion burned away inside her chest and she was powerless to snuff out the flame.

Besides, she didn't want to. Oh, there were twenty reasons why she shouldn't love Sloan, but she did. It had snared her like a rabbit. The rope was pulled tight around her leg now, the only thing to do was settle down. Struggling only pulled it tighter.

Voices touched her ears and she reached for her father's rifle instantly. A sarcastic smile twisted her lips as she handled the cold metal of the weapon. She might have fallen in love, but at least she was learning a few useful habits along the way.

The door was already unbarred, so she pulled it inward enough to peer out into the front drive. Her father's rifle firmly grasped in her right hand, she made sure to point the muzzle of the gun out the door before she showed her head.

A rare grin graced her husband's face as he took in the rifle. Warren stood holding his horse's reins as Jed tipped his hat to her. The ground was coated in white, fresh snow. The trees dusted in it. White clouds rose from the men's mouths as they spoke and they stomped at the ground to keep their legs warm.

"Warren and Jed will be moving into the mill house for the winter." Sloan stamped his boots on the front step to break off the snow crusted up to his ankles. The place instantly shrank with his huge frame inside. A little ripple of reaction filtered through her. Instant and uncontrollable. Her body responded to him without a single thought from her head.

"We rotate shifts on the dock. Along with a few other men. We'll plan on building a bunkhouse this spring so that you can mill when the river runs smooth."

Her lover had vanished just as completely as the night had. Sloan looked as dark and unmovable as he had the first time she'd run into him on the dock. The railroad agent was as solid as granite.

"It's freezing down there in the winter."

Sloan nodded agreement. "Nothing a stove can't fix. Warren and Jed are family of a sort." He watched her face for a reaction. "You'll get used to them."

His explanation was finished as he and Warren moved past her on their way back into the cabin. Sloan opened the door to her old bedroom. There was a rasp of wood against wood and then the smaller bed that had been hers tipped end first through the doorway. The men held only the frame, the thick padded mattress left rolled on the floor. The two men took it right out of the cabin and down the front step. She could see Jed moving around inside the mill house.

All three men were hard. A shiver worked over her back as she saw the twin rifles leaning up against the outside of the mill house. Setting her father's weapon aside, she hugged her arms close against the chill while her thoughts spun. She felt trapped in a fashion, but also secure. It was an odd tangle of emotions that surrounded her new love for the man at the center of it all. She didn't like a few things about him, but that didn't seem to change the fact that she loved him.

"Oh, bother!" Turning in a swirl of petticoats, she stomped into her cabin to cook breakfast. One thing the town gossips had right, men were completely foreign to a woman's way of thinking.

CR

"Don't be mad at me, honey."

Her temper lost a great deal of its heat as she listened to his voice. Oh, it was still firm and full of authority, but there was also an attempt to share his reasoning with her. Determination filled his eyes as she turned to stare at him.

"The sight of you shackled to that wall is branded into my mind. I think I just might go crazy if I have to worry about you out here all alone every shift. Warren and Jed are the closest kin I have, next to you now."

It was as much explanation as he was going to give her. Brianna saw it in his eyes. He cupped her chin as he moved closer. "I trust them with my life, but you're more important than that. I won't take the chance."

Understanding wiggled past her temper. The thought of being chained to Joseph's wall again made her shiver, too. It was a harsh truth, but she was lucky to have escaped. It wouldn't have been the first time a claim was stolen through a marriage. Locking stares with her husband, she offered him a small smile. "I believe the good reverend did mention something about learning to work together in a marriage."

"Yeah, he did. Give it a try for me." He pressed a kiss against her lips before releasing her. He pulled his hat from the nail he'd taken to hanging it on. As he pushed it down onto his head, she stared at the formal picture he made. The black duster and hat transforming him into that man who was invincible in her eyes. Maybe that was the true definition of love, unfaltering belief.

"You'll know I'm on my way back when Warren clears out to take charge on the dock." Something flashed in his eyes as he lingered in the doorframe. "But I will be back, Mrs. McAlister. Count on that."

"I believe I will, Mr. McAlister. I do hope you are up to the challenge. I have high expectations."

"I heard tell that wives are like that."

Brianna blew him a kiss. "You may depend upon it, Mr. McAlister."

Her teasing little voice kept him warm as he pulled his horse out of the small stable next to the mill house. Sloan felt a silly grin lift his lips as he saddled his horse. Brianna did that to him. She unlocked some kind of hidden door where he'd stockpiled his emotions over years of being alone. He saw her fussing around her kitchen as he rode past. Leaving took a little chunk out of his happiness, but he found himself looking forward to the return trip because she would be waiting for him.

So much more than lust. It was just possible that's what made a man face life with a smile on his face. Knowing that someone was waiting for him when he got home.

He sure was going to enjoy finding out.

CR

Over the next week, winter tightened its grip on Silver Peak. Brianna found herself enjoying snow more than she ever had before. Oh, she'd fallen all right and there wasn't even a single protest from her conscience to repent. She found herself ridiculously happy as she cooked supper every night, because she was feeding more than herself.

Checking the light outside, she shivered as she relatched the window. Sloan would be home soon. Reaching for her cornmeal, she placed some in a bowl and added lard and salt to begin fixing up some bread. Men ate a whole lot more than women did. Cooking for her father had sure taught her that.

A frown covered her face as her fingers froze on the fork. Her heart didn't want to let him go yet, but the facts were mounting against Gregory Spencer turning up alive. It seemed almost a sacrilege to be so happy when her father was likely dead on some patch of Arizona ground without even a decent burial. Shaking her melancholy thoughts aside, she finished the corn bread and placed it on the back of the stove to bake, making sure the lid of her large pot was in place to keep the heat inside the thick cast iron.

Three quick raps hit the front door, making her smile. It was a silly sort of expression that she giggled over as she went and tapped a single time in response. Two more raps shook the wood before she pulled the thick bar up to allow her husband inside. He blew in with a scattering of snow, the white flecks peppering the floor as he shrugged out of his duster.

"Hello, wife."

She wiggled against the kiss he pressed on her, pushing him away. "Your nose is cold!"

Sloan growled at her and captured her with one arm around her waist. He pulled her against his body, hugging her from behind. "So warm me up, honey."

His voice was dark with promise and it made her shiver. Anticipation bubbled up inside her as his hand smoothed down her belly to her hips. Turning her head, she pressed a slow kiss to his mouth, lingering over the touch of their lips as she enjoyed the rise of passion. His fingers flexed over each of her hips as she felt the hardening of his cock against her back.

"After supper."

A low grunt was her husband's reply. Brianna laughed at his disgruntlement before pulling at his hands to escape. "I'm tired of chipping off burnt food from my cooking pots, husband."

He huffed, but let her go. She caught the sound of his belly rumbling as the scent of their supper captured his attention. But he didn't sit down at the table for her to serve him a plate. Instead he clasped one of her wrists with his large hand and pulled her back into his embrace. This time she faced him and watched his eyes flicker with doubt. An emotion she wasn't accustomed to seeing on him. It snaked down into her heart, because somehow she knew that if he didn't care about her, she wouldn't see such a thing. Maybe she might never hear the words, but some things you knew without hearing.

Even if she did long for the words. A little sigh escaped her. Maybe it was just a woman's need, hearing that she was loved. Some kind of tender emotional desire that men didn't think about. The back of his hand stroked across her face as he considered her for a long moment.

"I have something for you." His eyes filled with indecision. "I was going to wait until Christmas, but I need to know."

The holiday was still over a month away and Brianna didn't much like the idea of waiting either. The last year of struggling to pay the land mortgage hadn't left any time for presents or even comforts. She couldn't even recall the last time she'd tasted a piece of sugar candy.

His fingers reached into his vest pocket. Whatever he withdrew, it was small, barely fitting on the tip of his smallest finger. The light from the lamp reflected off it as she looked closer. The slim gold band was polished to a high shine.

A little "oh" got caught on her lips. The few bits of jewelry her mother had owned had been sold to finance their move west. Getting married had never included a wedding ring, because laying down money for a decoration wasn't necessary. Coal stockpiled for winter was far more important.

Practicality. It was harder to chew on some days than others. Staring at the shiny circle of gold, Brianna choked on the dry facts of everyday living.

"You shouldn't have spent money on a ring." Disappointment laced her voice in spite of her best effort to stand firm in the face of her wants. She was mesmerized by the little bit of gold, her finger itching to try it on. But that was a childish, selfish emotion. Their money should be used for the important things they needed, not a silly woman's desire.

"I wanted to buy it for you."

There was hard purpose in his voice. He raised the gold band up in front of her face. "A wedding in front of a reverend is more legal than anything else. I'm asking you to wear my ring because I love you."

Her eyes welled up with tears that promptly tumbled right down her cheeks. Brianna didn't care one bit about the excessive emotion, because those three little words were bouncing around inside her head, drowning out every other detail in the world. The coal and the land mortgage and winter supplies were all just things. Love was eternal. She lifted her left hand and laughed at the tremor shaking it. Touching her ring finger to the tip of his pinky, she smiled through her tears at him.

"I thought you'd never get around to letting me love you."

His lips broke the stern mask he'd hidden his feelings behind. She watched them curl up as he pushed the little band down her finger. She held her breath as the warm metal slid smoothly into place. He closed his hand around hers as she caught the faint sparkle of unshed tears in his eyes. "If you ever stop loving me, take it off."

"I couldn't talk myself out of loving you on the second day we met, so don't count on it ever leaving my hand, Sloan McAlister."

"I'll be happy to take that bet, Brianna McAlister." He leaned towards her mouth, pressing a hard kiss to her lips as she forgot about the supper burning on her stove. The little golden band stayed firmly on her finger as her husband took her to bed and whispered his polished words of love against her bare body. Her fantasies paled in comparison as her heart absorbed the reality of hearing the word "love" in their bed. Now that was what little girls should dream about!

CR

They dined on corn bread—burnt on the bottom...again.

The snow had melted into a puddle on her floor and Brianna was too happy to care. Sloan's gaze followed her around the cabin as she set his overcooked supper in front of him and nibbled on the top of her share.

A horse nicker drifted in from the closed door, shattering the moment of intimacy. Sloan surged out of his seat in a tightly control motion. The rifle was already in his hand before he pushed her against the wall.

"Stay behind me."

There wasn't a hint of leniency in his voice. It was full of pure command as he stepped in front of her to open the door. Snow was falling in a gentle white shower, Sloan's tracks already covered in fresh powder. A single rider approached and Sloan's rifle lowered to aim its barrel right at him. The hands on the reins pulled the animal to a halt before the rider pushed the brim of his hat up to stare at them.

When she stuck her head through the doorway to peer into the dim light cast out from her lamp, her breath caught in her throat.

"No, don't shoot him." Her heart accelerated so fast, she had to gasp to keep enough air in her lungs. Sloan never took his eyes off the man sitting in the road. The muzzle of his rifle directly on his heart.

"That's my daddy."

Gregory Spencer was a lot plumper than she remembered. Brianna dived right under her husband's arm as he returned the rifle to his shoulder. She heard his snort of disapproval, but still ran through the shin-deep snow towards her father.

But when she hugged him her father also grunted with disapproval. His arm tightened around her as he glared at Sloan. Her husband had followed her across the drive and stood just out of reach of her father.

"You'd better be my son-in-law." Her daddy sounded madder than she ever remembered hearing him. He divided his attention between watching Sloan and looking at her.

"Sloan McAlister. We got married last week."

"I'll hear that from my daughter, if you don't mind." Her daddy lifted one eyebrow towards her. Brianna smiled and raised her hand. The snow tickled her skin as it fell, but her wedding band glistened. A twinkle lit her daddy's eyes as he looked at the smile on her face. He turned and offered his hand to Sloan as her husband met him in a firm handshake.

"Glad to hear it. There's plenty of work around here."

A wagon rattled behind them. Brianna watched as a buckboard turned the bend in the road. Her father lifted a gloved hand in greeting as he winked at her.

"That's your new stepmother I wrote you about."

Brianna gasped at her father's announcement. "I never got any letters, Daddy. Not a word."

Her father frowned. He glared at Sloan for a long moment before looking back at her. "Brianna Marie, why did you get married?"

The buckboard stopped and the horses tossed their head. Brianna smiled at her father as the world bloomed with every happy thing that she could possibly dream of having.

"Because I fell in love, Daddy. I fell in love."

A smile lifted her father's lips as he nodded approval. "Funny thing is, so did I, daughter."

❧

Spring

Sloan grinned as his wife snarled at him. Her arms were propped on her hips as her lip curled with her temper. It was the honest truth that he still enjoyed that spunk.

"Stop grinning at me, Sloan McAlister!"

He touched the brim of his hat in reply. "Then you'll have to stop looking so pretty, Mrs. McAlister."

"Ha!" She wasn't pretty! She was swollen up like a dairy cow. All she needed was a pail next to her feet to use when milking her and she still had three full months before her child was due. Her eyes stung as tears began to ease down her cheeks.

"Oh, bother!" She slapped her hands onto her skirt as she failed to control the surge of emotion—again. Not only did she look like a prize heifer, she acted like a baby, too. Her husband chuckled before capturing her against his body. He dusted her cheeks and nose with tiny kisses as she wriggled to escape. His hand caught the back of her neck to hold her steady as he stared into her eyes. Love shone in the dark orbs and it unleashed another few tears from her eyes.

"Love is the prettiest sight any man could ask for." The baby growing inside her kicked out against the hold his father had on her. Enjoyment sparkled in her husband's eyes as he felt the movement of their unborn child. A whistle sailed up from the new cabin her father was building. Sloan waggled his eyebrows before kissing her and turning towards the project. Her stepmother hummed as she made up the beds and the sound of wood being sawed filled the air as Sloan began to work alongside her father.

Her new house was pale gold in the early spring morning sun. The new lumber gleamed as Warren and Jed drove nails through it. Snow still lay in clumps on the ground and the river wasn't running ice-free yet. So her house was rising up before her baby made his appearance.

Her father's letters never did arrive, but his story sure filled a few cold winter nights. His new wife, Wind-Song, was Chinese, and if there was a frail bone in her compact body, Brianna had yet to discover it. The woman never raised her voice above a soft level, but she was pure stubborn determination. Brianna laughed every time she envisioned Clayton trying to avoid paying his mill fee. Her daddy claimed her step-mother's iron will was the reason he was still alive, Wind-Song's determination to have her way. She'd found him half-dead of a rattlesnake bite and refused to fetch him a preacher. Instead she'd filled him full of ancient Chinese medicine while wrapping his infected leg in foul-smelling herbs and roots. His letters home most likely were burned because they came from a Chinese boy, and race was still so important to some westerners. Even the post officers often refused to process mail handed over by non-whites. But just looking at her father and Wind-Song made her long for people who would leave love alone to sprout where it would.

"Come in and make clothes for baby, daughter."

Wind-Song poked her head through the open doorway. "You have no time once baby is born. Listen to Wind-Song, make baby clothes today."

A bolt of soft muslin fabric was already placed on the table, now that breakfast had been cleared away. The small cabin was bursting at its seams with family and Brianna decided it was absolutely perfect.

Even Joseph Corners earned a hint of gratitude from her as she recalled just how much the man had helped push her into Sloan's arms. A little giggle shook her as she began to cut a tiny nightshirt out for her baby. Yes, love did show up under the most mysterious of ways in the Spencer family. Rattlesnakes and claim jumpers, she could just imagine what lay in store for the coming season. Warren and Jed couldn't possibly understand what fate might cast their way.

The idea kept her smiling the rest of the day.

About the Author

To learn more about Mary Wine, please visit www.marywine.com. Send an email to talk2marywine@hotmail.com.

Look for these titles by Mary Wine

Now Available:

Evolution's Embers
Full Disclosure

*Passion flares between a federal marshal
and his enemy's wife.*

Another Man's Wife
© *2007 Denysé Bridger*

Outlaws descend on a stagecoach winding down its long journey between Missouri and Wind River, Wyoming. Federal Marshal Chris McQuade is one of the two occupants of the stage, and the ensuing battle leaves three dead men on the trail.

McQuade's unlikely partner in the deed is a woman he's been attracted to from the start of the trip. It isn't until they're forced to go on alone together that he realizes he's falling for the wife of the man he's been sent to bring to justice. Despite the ring on her finger and the role he plans to play in making her a widow, passion ignites and McQuade is surprised to discover that Elizabeth Davis is as helpless as he is to deny their need for each other.

But Elizabeth's husband has witnessed a much-too-intimate encounter between his enemy and his wife...and now he is out for revenge.

Available now in ebook from Samhain Publishing.

Enjoy the following excerpt from Another Man's Wife...

"Is this my horse?" she asked, inwardly shocked by the husky rasp of her voice. This was as close to Chris McQuade as she'd ever been, and it was an overwhelming experience for her senses. Awareness of him filled her; the mixed scents of man and horse, the mesmerizing depth of his dark eyes, the wind-ruffled disarray of his hair, and the sheer masculine strength that emanated from him. She wanted to touch him, to taste him, to feel his hands on her. The very thoughts made her weak in the knees.

Chris lifted his hat off the pommel of the saddle and stepped back to give her room to mount the gelding. She swung into the saddle with natural ease, and the seconds her bottom swayed before his face were almost his undoing. The next few days were going to be painfully long, some inner voice warned as he tried to ignore the surge of lust that shot straight to his groin. He pulled his hat low and went to the second horse, settling on the saddle and turning west without another word. By the time she came alongside him, he was reasonably certain he could safely look at her.

Elizabeth's eyes drank in the beauty of the landscape around them. The Wind River Mountains loomed far in the distance and it was difficult to judge just how far away the town might be. "How long before we reach Wind River?"

"Likely be a few days," Chris replied, peering intently ahead. "We're going to have to ride hard to get to the foothills, then head north. Town shouldn't be too hard to find from there."

"Have you been there before?" She moved easily with the horse, well accustomed to riding. The gelding was a spirited animal, and she felt an affinity for him already. She suspected he'd move like the wind if the need arose, and she named him Wind Dancer in her mind, smiling at the whimsy.

Chris obviously caught the expression and she enjoyed the telltale tug at the corner of his mouth as he watched her with open amusement.

"Somethin' funny goin' on, ma'am?" he said, the natural drawl flowing into his voice again.

She shook her head and bit back the grin that wanted to spread over her features. "Nothing funny, Mr. McQuade," she assured him, then urged Wind Dancer into an exhilarating gallop, leaning over the pommel of the saddle and reveling in the movement of the horse beneath her. Only seconds later she heard him closing the distance between them. Instead of censure or the anger she anticipated, Chris whooped loudly as he passed her and she laughed with pure pleasure and let her horse's gait open up further. The two animals were well-matched for strength and speed and it was a long while before Chris slowed and pointed to a copse of trees less than a mile ahead.

"We'll make camp there for the night," he told her when she drew up next to him.

The sun was sinking rapidly on the western peaks of the mountains and the color streaked the sky with a splendor unlike any she'd seen before. She stared, enchanted and enthralled by the fiery display that crested the snow-capped mountaintops. The orange-gold orb of heavenly fire gradually dipped behind the ridge of darkening mountains, its last searching fingers splaying over the tops, turning everything to purple tinted pink. Chris nudged his horse forward and she followed, caught between the glory atop the mountains and the magnificence of the man and horse moving ahead of her.

Less than an hour later they sat in front of a fire, coffee brewing and filling the night air with its enticing aroma. They shared some of the hard tack and jerked beef from Tom Caden's saddlebags, and Elizabeth felt a rare moment of tranquility as she gazed upward at the glittering sky. The moon was making a slow climb into the center of the tapestry of black velvet that draped over them, its silvery crescent growing brighter and brighter.

"What exactly do you do, Chris?" She finally dared ask the question she'd been thinking about from the first time she'd glimpsed him back in St. Louis.

One bashful lady discovers her dashing husband might be a traitor to their country.

One Bashful Lady
© 2007 Brenda Williamson

Desmond Rawlington, Marquess of Dunsmore and seductive charmer, needs a Delacorte sister as a wife. When the eldest elopes, Desmond marries Ainsley only to find himself falling in love with the enchanting young woman, despite her quirky habit of hiding behind draperies.

Lady Ainsley Delacorte, the shyest person anyone has ever met, is nervous around servants, overwhelmed by the ton and forced into marriage. Her reluctance fades with her husband's sinfully romantic touch, but she can't forget he's involved in a traitorous plot to return Napoleon to power.

When Ainsley is caught with an incriminating letter she stole from her husband, Desmond intervenes. Will they face the gallows or can love save them?

Available now in ebook and print from Samhain Publishing.